W9-BDW-128

*As if he could not help himself,
his lips came down on hers.*

For a moment Oletha could hardly believe it was happening. Then she knew that from what had been a hell of fear, she had been lifted into a Heaven of happiness she had not even known existed.

As the Duke took possession of her lips she realised that this was what she had been wanting and longing for—she knew now that she had fallen in love with him the moment she had seen him.

Books by Barbara Cartland

A SONG OF LOVE
MONEY, MAGIC AND MARRIAGE
A HAZARD OF HEARTS
DESIRE OF THE HEART
THE COIN OF LOVE
THE ENCHANTING EVIL
LOVE IN HIDING
CUPID RIDES PILLION
THE UNPREDICTABLE BRIDE
A DUEL OF HEARTS
LOVE IS THE ENEMY
THE HIDDEN HEART
LOVE TO THE RESCUE
LOVE HOLDS THE CARDS
LOST LOVE
LOVE IS CONTRABAND
THE KNAVE OF HEARTS
LOVE ME FOREVER
THE SMUGGLED HEART
THE CAPTIVE HEART
SWEET ADVENTURE
THE GOLDEN GONDOLA
THE LITTLE PRETENDER
STARS IN MY HEART (also published as STARS IN HER EYES)
THE SECRET FEAR
MESSENGER OF LOVE
THE WINGS OF LOVE
THE ENCHANTED WALTZ
THE HIDDEN EVIL
A VIRGIN IN PARIS
A KISS OF SILK
LOVE IS DANGEROUS
THE KISS OF THE DEVIL
THE RELUCTANT BRIDE
THE UNKNOWN HEART
ELIZABETHAN LOVER
WE DANCED ALL NIGHT
AGAIN THIS RAPTURE
THE ENCHANTED MOMENT
THE KISS OF PARIS
THE PRETTY HORSE-BREAKERS
OPEN WINGS
LOVE UNDER FIRE
NO HEART IS FREE
STOLEN HALO
THE MAGIC OF HONEY
LOVE IS MINE
THE AUDACIOUS ADVENTURESS

BARBARA CARTLAND'S BOOK OF BEAUTY & HEALTH
WINGS ON MY HEART
A HALO FOR THE DEVIL
LIGHTS OF LOVE
SWEET PUNISHMENT
A GHOST IN MONTE CARLO
LOVE IS AN EAGLE
LOVE ON THE RUN
LOVE FORBIDDEN
BLUE HEATHER
A LIGHT TO THE HEART
LOST ENCHANTMENT
THE PRICE IS LOVE
SWEET ENCHANTRESS
OUT OF REACH
THE IRRESISTIBLE BUCK
THE COMPLACENT WIFE
THE ODIOUS DUKE
PASSIONATE PILGRIM
THE THIEF OF LOVE
THE DREAM WITHIN
ARMOUR AGAINST LOVE
A HEART IS BROKEN
THE RUNAWAY HEART
THE LEAPING FLAME
AGAINST THE STREAM
THEFT OF A HEART
WHERE IS LOVE?
TOWARDS THE STARS
A VIRGIN IN MAYFAIR
DANCE ON MY HEART
THE ADVENTURER
A RAINBOW TO HEAVEN
LOVE AND LINDA
DESPERATE DEFIANCE
LOVE AT FORTY
THE BITTER WINDS OF LOVE
BROKEN BARRIERS
LOVE IN PITY
THIS TIME IT'S LOVE
ESCAPE FROM PASSION
METTERNICH THE PASSIONATE DIPLOMAT
JOSEPHINE EMPRESS OF FRANCE
THE SCANDALOUS LIFE OF KING CAROL
WOMAN THE ENIGMA
ELIZABETH EMPRESS OF AUSTRIA

BARBARA CARTLAND

6

MONEY, MAGIC AND MARRIAGE

A JOVE BOOK

Copyright © 1980 by Barbara Cartland

All rights reserved. No part of this publication may be reproduced or transmitted in any form or by any means, electronic or mechanical, including photocopy, recording, or any information storage and retrieval system, without permission in writing from the publisher.

Requests for permission to make copies of any part of the work should be mailed to: Permissions, Jove Publications, Inc., 200 Madison Avenue, New York, NY 10016

First Jove edition published October 1980

10 9 8 7 6 5 4 3 2 1

Printed in the United States of America

Jove books are published by Jove Publications, Inc.,
200 Madison Avenue, New York, NY 10016

The Geneva version of the English Bible, published by Christopher Barker in 1576, is now in the library of the University of Chicago. The First Folio of Shakespeare's plays, dated 1623, is in the Folger Shakespeare Library.

Every important home in England in the seventeenth and eighteenth centuries had large libraries; and first editions, which have been lost or forgotten down the centuries, are still being found on their shelves.

At Longleat, the lovely house of the Marquis of Bath, I was recently shown two Ships' logs written by Sir Francis Drake.

Many libraries were, of course, sold, and those dispersed by the famous Harleian collection and that of Sir Hans Sloane, became part of the newly founded British Museum in 1750.

In the eighteenth century for the first time a group of wealthy Englishmen began systematically to collect early printed books. These pioneers included the 1st and 2nd Earls of Oxford, the 3rd Earl of Sutherland, the 1st Duke of Roxburgh, the 8th Earl of Pembroke and the 2nd Duke of Devonshire.

The greatest collector of the generation was the 2nd Earl of Spenser, whose books were headed by 56 Caxtons and the first editions of the Greek and Latin classics.

My daughter is now married to the 8th Earl, and although there are some lovely and valuable books at Althorp in Northampton, the 2nd Earl's collection became, in 1892, the nucleus of the John Rylands Library in Manchester.

MONEY, MAGIC AND MARRIAGE

Chaper One

1898

COLONEL ASHURST put down the letter he was reading with a smile of triumph.

"I have won!" he exclaimed.

His daughter Oletha looked up from the other side of the table to say:

"I did not know you had a horse racing this week, Papa."

"Not a horse," the Colonel replied, "but something far more important."

Oletha waited.

She knew her father liked to tell a story in his own time, and she was aware it was something very pleasant by the expression on his face.

Colonel Ashurst was still an extremely good-looking man and in his youth he had been so

1

handsome that, as her mother had told Oletha, every girl had fallen in love with him.

"When I arrived in England from America," she had said in her soft musical voice that only very occasionally held a touch of an accent, "I was expecting Englishmen to be good-looking, but when I saw your father I was overwhelmed."

"Where did you first see him, Mama?" Oletha had asked.

"At the first Ball I had ever been to in England," her mother had replied. "It actually was a Hunt Ball and it was fascinating for me to see all the gentlemen in their pink tail-coats with lapels in the colour of the Hunt to which they belonged. But I was a little shocked at how boisterous they were."

Oletha laughed.

She had always heard, although she had never been to one, that at Hunt Balls in the early hours of the morning, the lancers, the polka, and the gallop got a little out of hand.

"But you enjoyed yourself, Mama?" she asked.

"Immensely! But when I met your father I knew something had happened to me! I had never expected to fall in love with an Englishman."

"Was it such a terrible thing to do?"

"My father and mother thought so. They brought me to England because they themselves were curious about the country in which their ancestors had originated, but they had no wish to leave me here and they did everything they could to persuade me to return to America."

"But once you fell in love with Papa it was impossible for you to go away," Oletha said, having heard the story before.

"He has always sworn that he would never have let me go and even if I tried to do so, he would have kidnapped me and forced me to marry him however much I protested."

Oletha thought this was very much in line with her father's rather buccaneering attitude towards anything he wanted.

He was always determined to be the victor, and it was this characteristic which had made him first a very good soldier and secondly a successful race-horse owner.

She thought now it must have been one of the horses which made him look so pleased.

As she waited he said:

"You know I have always had great ambitions for you, Oletha."

"What sort of ambitions, Papa?"

She thought then it must have something to do with her education, because unlike most English fathers, he had always wanted her to be clever.

She knew it was partly the fact that she was an only child.

Although he would seldom admit it, the Colonel was desperately disappointed that he had not had a son to carry on the Ashurst name in the house which had belonged to the family for four hundred years.

But because he would never be defeated, he had brought Oletha up to excel in many activities that were generally the perquisite of men.

Under his tuition she became not only an outstanding rider, but also an excellent game-shot.

In the hunting-field she was invariably "in at the kill," and although it would have been too outrageous for her to shoot with the guns when her father had a party, he would often arrange a special shoot just for her, himself, the Estate Agent, and one of his old and trusted comrades.

Sometimes Oletha knew that when, because her eye was so accurate, she brought down a particularly high pheasant or a partridge at long range, the old gentlemen were quite annoyed.

Apart from this she had the best tutors in all the subjects at which any intelligent man would have wanted his son to excel.

Oletha had therefore learnt Greek and Latin, and her father would sometimes say almost wistfully that it was a pity that she could not go to Oxford where it was certain she would have been an outstanding success.

When she told him there was a women's College at the University sacred to men, her father had told her in no uncertain terms, that no daughter of his would be anything but a feminine woman.

This was a contradiction to which he had introduced her almost as soon as she was old enough to understand serious subjects, and strangely enough she had achieved the impossible and surprised him by being exactly as he wanted her to be.

She certainly looked very feminine now from the other side of the breakfast-table.

Slim, graceful, at the same time with an athletic, co-ordinated body from the amount of exercise she took, Oletha was unusually lovely.

She had huge eyes which, when she was angry or emotionally aroused, seemed almost the colour of pansies.

They were a complement to the colour of her hair, which thanks to some far off Swedish ancestor who had made his way into America a century earlier, was the gold of ripening corn.

Also from the other side of the Atlantic had come the strong little chin that could at times make her as determined as her father.

Most people, however, found themselves noticing only the loveliness in her eyes and the straight classical little nose that lay between them.

It seemed to Oletha that her father looked at her in a strangely scrutinising manner before he said:

"My ambitions, my dearest, concern your marriage."

Oletha's eyes widened and she could not have looked more astonished than if her father had dropped a bombshell on the table.

"My . . . marriage, Papa?"

"It is something I have not mentioned before," the Colonel answered, "because you are so young and I was planning that next year you would have a Season in London, and of course be presented at Court. But something has happened now which had made me change my plans."

"What is . . . that?" Oletha asked, because she knew it was expected of her.

She was feeling as if her father had dealt her an unexpected blow and she was finding it difficult to think clearly.

She had expected that he would plan every other aspect of her life, especially since her mother's death, but she had thought the possibility of marriage was so far in the future that she seldom even gave it a passing thought.

She was aware that he thought this last Season when she was only seventeen that she was too young to be a debutante and had been quite content to wait until next April when she would be nearly eighteen-and-a-half.

There were so many things to do on their estate in Worcestershire and so many horses to ride, that she was in no hurry to embark on the hectic round of Balls, Receptions and other festivities which were an inseparable part of a debut.

She had thought, however, that with her father beside her it would be fun, but now he had other ideas.

"You will remember, Oletha," the Colonel was saying, "that I have often spoken to you of my friendship with the Duke of Gorleston?"

"Yes, of course, Papa. I remember how you told me that you met him some years ago at Epsom, and that he was extremely grateful because you told him to back your horse which was an outsider, and it won."

"That is true," the Colonel answered, "and after that whenever we met on the race-course the Duke would always come up to me and say:

"'Have you a good tip for me today, Ashurst? I am relying on you to send me home with some guineas in my pocket.'"

"I am sure you never failed him, Papa."

"Not often," the Colonel agreed, "and because I was able to help the Duke when he needed it, we became friends, which needless to say I found very gratifying."

Oletha looked surprised because she thought it was a strange way for her father to speak, and because they were so close to each other he understood what she was feeling and explained:

"Dukes, my dear child, are a race apart, and yet I have always maintained that sport makes all men equal. That has certainly been true where I am concerned."

7

"I do not think I understand, Papa."

Colonel Ashurst took a sip of coffee from the cup beside him before he replied:

"Let me explain, and as it happens it is very pertinent to what I am going to say to you later."

"I am listening, Papa."

"The Ashursts, as you are aware, are a well-known family here in Worcestershire where our ancestors have lived in this very house for generations. My father and my grandfather before him, served in the Worcestershire Yeomanry, and we have filled many official appointments in the County with the exception of that of Lord Lieutenant."

"I have often wondered why that post was not offered to you, Papa."

"I can answer that quite simply," the Colonel replied. "I am not important enough! The Lord Lieutenant represents Her Majesty the Queen, and although we have every reason to be proud of our lineage and of being acknowledged as gentlefolk, we are not in the real sense of the world aristocrats."

Oletha gave a little laugh.

"Does it trouble you, Papa?"

"Not in the slightest where I am concerned."

Her father paused looking at her in a way which made her know instinctively that he was thinking of her.

Then he continued:

"My father was not a wealthy man, nor was I, but when I married your mother because I loved her, I found long after I had proposed, that she was by English standards a considerable heiress."

"Mama has often told me how surprised you were," Oletha smiled, "and she told me that, because you were so proud, it was hard to convince you that it did not matter if she had more money than you had."

"Of course I minded," the Colonel admitted, "but whether your mother was penniless or as rich as Croesus it was of no consequence beside the fact that we loved each other."

Oletha clasped her hands together.

"Oh, Papa, it is so romantic! I have always hoped that I would meet someone like you and fall in love in the same way."

She saw her father glance down at the letter that lay on the table. Then he said:

"Perhaps that is asking too much, my dearest. Love at first sight happens perhaps only once in a million times, and I have always been exceedingly grateful that I was fortunate enough to experience it."

For a moment he sat staring across the room as if he was looking back into the past and the happiness he had known with his American bride.

"Go on, Papa, with what you were saying," Oletha prompted him.

With a start his eyes came back to her and he said:

"There is no need for me to remind you that while your mother and I were well off when we first married, it was not until five years ago when your American grandfather's oil wells were discovered that we became really wealthy."

"I remember the excitement when the letter came telling you that Mama was now a multi-millionairess," Oletha said, "and yet it seemed after the first excitement was over to make very little difference."

"That is true," her father agreed. "You see, Oletha, we had everything we wanted: each other and you, our very adorable daughter. So the only thing we really spent your mother's fortune on, apart from putting in a number of bathrooms, was horses."

"The Ashurst Stud is now famous," Oletha said, with just a slightly mocking note in her voice."

"So it ought to be!" the Colonel said. "I bought the best and after years of studying, breeding, and training horses myself, and not leaving it just to those I could pay, my theories, you have to admit, have come off."

This, his daughter knew, was a source of great pride to him, and she said quickly:

"No-one could have been more successful than you have, Papa. Everybody agrees that you are more knowledgeable than any other owner in the Jockey Club."

"How do you know that?" the Colonel asked.

"I read it in the *Sporting Times*."

"You must show it to me," her father said. "It is the sort of thing a man likes to have said about him."

Then as if he realised the discussion had wandered from Oletha to himself, he said in a different tone:

"But we were talking about you. After your beloved mother died I realised that I had to look after you alone, and I began to think very seriously about your future."

"Almost as if I were one of your horses!" Oletha said, with a twinkle in her eye, but her father ignored the interruption.

"Every woman wants to be married and every father, if he loves his daughter, wants to see her married to a man with whom she will not only be happy, but who can give her a position in the social world which will command respect."

Oletha did not speak but she was listening intently as her father went on:

"You will understand, my dearest, that being a racing man, I would like to see you first past the winning-post in the matrimonial stakes and watch you being awarded the finest trophy possible."

"The Gold Cup at Ascot, for instance!"

Oletha spoke lightly. At the same time, she was beginning to feel rather perturbed.

She did not like the way her father was talking of her marriage as if he had already arranged it, without even consulting her.

Although she seldom, if ever, opposed him, she was already determined that where her marriage was concerned it would be a matter of her decision and not his.

"You are taking a long time to come to the point, Papa," she said aloud. "Are you trying to say that you have already chosen my husband for me?"

Because she was a little afraid of the answer, the question was spoken in a voice that was louder than normal, and seemed for the moment to echo round the walls of the Morning-Room.

Her father's eyes met hers and she knew he intended to answer her bluntly and without further prevarication.

"Yes," he said, "I have made up my mind that you shall marry the new Duke of Gorleston!"

His reply was so surprising that Oletha gave a little gasp. Then she said:

"The *new* Duke? I did not know you had met him."

"He arrived from India just before Goodwood Races," the Colonel replied. "I think that before I spoke to him somebody had told him I was a friend of his father's and he greeted me most effusively."

12

He smiled as if it had pleased him and went on:

"Since then we have met on various occasions, but it was only when I was talking to him at Doncaster that I became aware of the position in which he finds himself now that he has inherited the title."

"And what is that, Papa?" Oletha asked, knowing almost before her father spoke what the answer would be.

"He is in desperate need of money."

She might have known, Oletha thought, that the whole conversation was leading up to this, but somehow now the words had been spoken they came as a distinct shock.

She had been aware that she was "handicapped," which was the actual word she used to herself, by the fortune which set her apart from other girls of her own age and which created in many ways, a barrier that she found it hard to bridge.

Even at the parties she had attended over the last few years with her contemporaries, she had heard the whispers amongst the Dowagers when she came into the room: "Of course, she is immensely wealthy!" while her own special friends were quite outspoken about it.

"It is not fair, Oletha," one of them had exclaimed only a few weeks ago, "that you are not only far more beautiful than anyone else, but also so rich."

"They are two things I cannot actually help," Oletha replied.

"Yes, I know," her friends had said, "and that makes it even more infuriating than it is already!"

They had laughed, but Oletha had been aware that there had been just a touch of envy that she hated to hear, and in the minds of other people there was often not only envy, but also malice.

"Never worry about having money, my darling," her mother had said to her, "except that you must be kinder, more generous, and more understanding to those who are without it."

"I do not quite understand, Mama," Oletha had said.

"Let me explain," her mother replied. "Because you are rich, people will always be a little jealous and perhaps try to take advantage of you. But it must never make you cynical or, even if they defraud you, bitter."

"Of course not," Oletha had murmured.

"You have to realise that it is a privilege to be able to help other people," her mother went on. "What is far more important than money is giving yourself in the way of sympathy, understanding, and love. Those are the things that really matter in life, and the mere fact that your grandfather has worked hard and been very lucky and accumulated a fortune, is no particular credit to you, but a responsibility you cannot ignore."

"I understand, Mama," Oletha said solemnly.

"It is not always easy to be rich, although people think it is what they most want in life," Mrs. Ashurst had gone on. "But trust your heart, Oletha."

"My heart?" Oletha had questioned.

"Yes," her mother answered. "Your heart will tell you whether the people who approach you are genuine and true, or pretentious and evil. Remember too the most valuable thing in the whole world is not money, but love."

Oletha remembered her mother's words now and she said quietly in a voice that was strictly controlled:

"Are you seriously asking me, Papa, to marry a man I have never seen? I cannot believe that you could ever suggest anything so outrageous to the Duke himself."

"Not exactly in so many words," her father said a little uncomfortably. "Let me tell you what happened."

"I am very anxious to hear it," Oletha said.

"We met in the Jockey Club Stand and I thought the Duke seemed pleased to see me. He does not know many people in England because he has been abroad, I learned, for nearly seven years."

"With his Regiment in India."

"Exactly! I believe he distinguished himself on the North-West Frontier and was mentioned in dispatches."

There was an undoubted note of triumph in

15

the Colonel's voice, since anything that concerned the Army always meant something personal to him.

"I asked the Duke," he continued, "what horses he had in training and he said:

"'As a matter of fact I was going to speak to you about that, Colonel Ashurst, because I need your advice.'

"'I am more than willing to help in any way I can,' I replied.

"'Then let me put it bluntly,' the Duke said. 'I cannot afford to keep up my father's racing-stable and I want you to tell me what is the best way to dispose of it.'"

"You can imagine," the Colonel said, looking across the table at Oletha, "I was completely stunned! The idea of no longer seeing the Gorleston horses taking part in the Classic races really shocked me!"

He gave a sigh before he added;

"The late Duke was so proud of his stable and when he won a race he was as excited as any schoolboy. It was a delight to see him."

"Did you know he had difficulties before he died, Papa?"

Her father looked a little embarrassed and she exclaimed before he could speak:

"You *did* know and you helped him!"

"It was easier for me to lend him money than for him to go to money-lenders," her father said as if excusing himself.

"It was kind of you, Papa. At the same time, I am sure you were glad to be able to help somebody you thought of as a friend."

Her father was always generous to his friends, Oletha knew, and it would please him in a special way to be able to help one not only because he had had an affection and admiration for him, but also because he was a Duke.

She could hear her mother's voice saying to her in the past with a hint of amusement in it:

"All the English are snobs, darling, as you will find out for yourself when you grow older, and there is not an Englishman born who does not truly love a Lord."

Oletha knew her father must have been delighted when his money, of which he had plenty, assisted anyone as important as the Duke of Gorleston.

"Go on with your story, Papa," she prompted for the second time.

"We found somewhere quiet in the Stand where we could talk," her father began, "and the new Duke told me of the conditions he had found now he had returned home. His father was in debt for quite a considerable amount, and what was worse, the estate has been neglected and the house is in desperate need of repairs, which should have been carried out years ago."

"You have always told me it is one of the finest houses in England," Oletha remarked.

"So it is, to look at," her father agreed, "and

I must admit when I stayed there, which was only once, I was too impressed by the contents to worry if the roof leaked or the ceilings were likely to fall down."

"You mean the pictures and furniture are very valuable? Then why does not the new Duke sell them?"

"Because they are entailed," her father replied. "In all great ancestral homes the contents, as well as the house and the estate itself, are not the property of the current holder, but are entailed from generation to generation from the past to the future, and there are Trustees who see that the place is handed down without depletion from each Duke in turn, to his son."

Oletha did not speak. She was beginning to understand exactly what her father had in mind.

He glanced at her speculatively before he went on:

"I talked to the Duke for a long time, and because he was obviously anxious to continue the conversation he asked me to meet him in London after the races were over and we had both returned home."

"So you saw him last night."

"He dined with me because he told me frankly he could not afford to open Gorleston House in Park Lane, and in fact, is closing completely several of his other houses."

There was silence, then the Colonel said:

"As soon as the Duke told me exactly what his position was, he finished by saying:

"'Because you were such a good friend of my father's I feel you will help me to sell what has to be sold without there being too much publicity in the newspapers or criticism of my father, for letting things get as bad as they are.'"

Oletha smiled and the Colonel added:

"I respected him for that. It was the way I would want my own son to feel if I were in a similar position."

Oletha knew that her father's being in such straits was unlikely, if not impossible, but she did not say so. She only waited and Colonel Ashurst went on:

"It was then I said to the Duke:

"'I have a better idea than your selling possessions which I know, because they are part of your family tradition, mean a great deal to you. It is that you should do what all great families have done, that is, marry an heiress to enable you to preserve the prestige of the Gorlestons and to keep what they have treasured for centuries intact.'"

Oletha drew in her breath.

"What did the Duke say?" she enquired.

"I realised I had, for the moment, surprised him," the Colonel answered. "I am sure that it had never struck him that was a solution to his difficulties."

19

"And then?"

"Then he said almost harshly:

"'I have a rooted objection, Colonel, to being a fortune-hunter!'

"'I can understand that,' I replied. 'At the same time, if you think it out, it is a sensible and actually a time-honoured way of meeting one's obligations and responsibilities.'

"He said nothing, and I went on:

"'You must think not only of yourself and your own feelings, but of all the many pensioners who I know will suffer if you cannot look after them as your father and grandfather and their fathers before them did at Gore, and on your father's other estates.'

"The Duke frowned, and I know this aspect had been in his mind and he had been wondering what he could do about it."

"'There are also,' I continued, 'the Orphan-ages, the Alms Houses, and the servants who have been in your family's employment from father to son all down the generations.'

"'I am well aware of what you are saying,' the Duke interrupted, 'but the idea of choosing a woman because she has money, and selling my title appalls me! I think it degrading and, if the word is not too strong, obscene!'

"He spoke sharply," Colonel Ashurst said, "and I knew because he is an extremely attractive man, that there must have been many women in

20

his life who had loved him for himself and not because he was the son of a Duke."

He paused before he added:

"Actually the possibility of his succeeding his father did not arise until a year ago."

"Why not?" Oletha enquired.

"Because he had an older brother."

"I had forgotten, if you have ever told me about him."

"As it happens, I never met him," the Colonel said. "He was in ill-health and spent his time going from spa to spa in Europe."

"What was wrong with him?"

"I really do not know. In fact, now I think of it, the old Duke seldom mentioned him, and I have never met anyone who knew the late Marquess."

"But he died."

Her father nodded.

"I knew when I saw the Duke after his older son's death, he was glad that his second son, Sandor, would now be the heir."

"I wonder if Sandor was glad or sorry," Oletha murmured almost to herself.

"The new Duke told me he had never expected to inherit," Colonel Ashurst replied, "nor had he ever been accorded any particular privilege as a Duke's son."

The Colonel's lips twisted a little wryly as he said:

"I knew exactly what he meant. In most aris-
tocratic families everything is concentrated on
the heir and the rest scrape along with very little
money and very little attention paid to them."

"It seems unfair," Oletha said.

"That is what your mother used to say," her
father answered, "but it is the English way of life
and whatever we may feel about it, we shall not
change it."

"No, of course not," Oletha said.

She thought to herself if she ever had any
children she certainly would see that her money
was divided fairly amongst them.

Then she remembered that if she married an
Englishman he would have complete control of
her fortune, and she would have no say in what
was done with it.

It suddenly struck her how very attractive a
poor man would find the prospect of marrying
her, especially if, like the Duke, he was in desperate need of money, not only for himself, but
for a great many other people as well.

"What did you say to the Duke about me,
Papa?" she asked, and the words were a challenge
she threw across the breakfast table.

"I said to him: 'I am not suggesting that you
should go fortune-hunting, and I quite understand
how the mere idea is repulsive to you, but I would
like you to meet my daughter.'"

"What did he answer to that?"

"He looked at me in surprise, because I am

sure he had no idea I had a daughter. He was aware your mother had died because I had told him I was a widower when he asked if I was alone at Goodwood."

"And what did you say about me?"

"Nothing!" her father answered, to her surprise. "I said to him: 'My daughter has not yet had a Season in London but has been brought up very quietly in the country. She is a very great heiress. Her grandfather was American and before he died he was known as the "Oil King of Texas".'

"'That is something I had not heard,' the Duke said briefly.

"'What I am going to suggest,' I went on, 'is that when you have thought over my suggestion, you will allow me to bring my daughter to stay with you at Gore. We could come as just ordinary guests when you have a party, and you can judge for yourself whether my idea would or would not solve your difficulties.'"

"And what did the Duke answer to that?" Oletha asked.

"He paused before he said: 'I will think over what you have said to me, Colonel, and when I have done so, I will write to you.'

"'You are returning to the country?' I asked.

"'I want to have another look at Gore,' he said, 'and go deeper into the state of affairs there. May I, until you hear from me, ask you to treat everything I have told you in confidence?'

23

" 'Of course,' I replied."

Oletha looked at her father across the table.

"I presume then, Papa, that the letter you now hold in your hand is what you have been waiting to receive from the Duke."

"It is indeed," Colonel Ashurst agreed. "It contains an invitation for you and me to join a house-party he is arranging for a shoot in two weeks time."

"A shoot!" Oletha exclaimed.

"The shoots at Gore are famous," her father explained. "The Prince of Wales was a frequent guest in the old Duke's days, and it is not surprising if the present Duke has been pressured into inviting His Royal Highness for the opening of the pheasant season."

"Surely a large house-party is something the Duke cannot afford!" Oletha exclaimed.

"You have forgotten the ramifications of sport," her father answered. "The pheasants for this season's shoot have already been reared and tended by the game-keepers during the summer months. Two months ago they will have been let loose into the woods."

He paused.

"After all that trouble it would be wrong to leave them unshot, besides being a waste of money, because the rearing of pheasants is an expensive business."

"Now I think about it, I understand that," Oletha said.

24

"You will have the privilege of seeing at Gore one of the best shoots in the country, and I do not mind admitting it is something I shall look forward to eagerly," Colonel Ashurst said. "I only wish you could shoot too, and show the Duke how well you handle a gun."

"Do you think that is the sort of accomplishment he would appreciate?" Oletha asked.

There was no doubt the question was sarcastic and her father looked at her sharply before he replied:

"Are you disliking or resenting the idea of marrying the man I have chosen for you?"

"Both!" Oletha said quickly. "Quite frankly, Papa, I feel as if you are selling me across the counter of a shop, and I find that distinctly humiliating."

Colonel Ashurst made a gesture with his hand.

"You know that is not how I wish you to feel!" he said almost angrily. "I am well aware that you would want to choose your own husband and fall in love, as I fell in love with your mother. But you are an intelligent girl, Oletha. Have you ever asked yourself if such a thing is possible?"

"What do you mean by that?"

"I mean that because you are so rich," her father said, "you will find the the average decent English gentleman will never ask you to be his wife."

He meant to startle his daughter, and he succeeded.

"But if I fell in love with him . . ." Oletha began.

"He would run a hundred miles rather than allow himself to fall in love with you," the Colonel interrupted before she could finish her sentence.

Oletha's eyes were very wide and he went on:

"The English have a rooted objection to being subservient to their wives, and so do real men the world over. If the woman is as rich as you are, Oletha, however attractive she may be, they take every precaution not to become involved with her in case she entices them into matrimony."

"But you . . . married Mama," Oletha faltered.

"As you are well aware, I would not have done so had she been as rich as you are, and I fell in love with her before I realised she was anything but an ordinary, well-to-do American who could afford to travel."

Oletha rose from the table and walked across the room to the window.

Despite the fact that she was wearing a riding-habit with the skirt looped up on one hip, she moved with a grace that was unusual in a young women and her hair, when it caught the light, was very lovely in contrast to the darkness of her riding-coat.

Her father watched her with an expression of pain in his eyes. He knew how vulnerable she was and he knew too, how hard life could be for a woman who was as rich as she was.

He had seen the fortune-hunters, the hangers-on, the men who chased women of all ages if they were rich, and he had sworn many years ago that he would fight with every means in his power to prevent his own daughter from being exploited by such despicable creatures. But he had told himself it was not going to be easy.

The young Duke, however, was the type of man, quite apart from his title, whom he would like to have as a son-in-law, if he could persuade first him, then Oletha, to accept the solution that he knew was the answer to both their problems.

Oletha did not speak and after a moment he said:

"When you meet the Duke you will know why I think he is the right type of man for you to have as a husband. He has seen life, has lived with danger and has learnt not only how to command men, but also himself."

She was still silent and he went on:

"What I am asking you to do, my dearest, is to meet him and make up your own mind. But as I have told you frankly and, if you like, brutally, you have not a wide choice. In fact, I would rather see you dead than married to the type of social waster who will woo you with flattering words merely so that he can get his greedy hands on your money."

27

The Colonel spoke so violently that Oletha turned round in surprise. Then as she saw the expression on his face she moved from the window to stand beside his chair and put her arm around his shoulders.

"You are upsetting yourself, Papa," she said. "Why do you not forget the whole idea of my marrying anyone? I am very happy to stay with you and you would miss me if I were no longer here."

She spoke coaxingly and when her father did not reply she bent down to lay her cheek against his.

"Have you forgotten our plans for hunting together this season?" she asked in a soft voice. "As Master of the Croome Hounds, you need me. You have always said that I am as good as two Whipper-ins."

The Colonel smiled and put up his hand to cover hers where it lay on his shoulder.

"Of course I would miss you," he said, "and the house would seem empty if you were no longer in it. But dearest, I may not always be here to protect you. Then what would happen?"

"You are still a young man, Papa, and you have many years in which to enjoy yourself."

"What a woman needs is a home of her own, a husband, and of course, children," the Colonel argued.

Oletha gave a little shudder as if the idea frightened her and he went on quickly:

"Trust me, let me do things my way. If I am beaten at the post, then I will accept defeat gracefully although I should be disappointed not to be the winner."

Oletha gave a little laugh as if she could not help herself. At the same time, her father was aware that the sound was not a happy one.

"Trust me," he said again.

Oletha straightened herself and took her arm from around his neck.

"Very well, Papa," she said. "I will go with you to Gore and look at your Duke. But you must promise me on all you hold sacred that you will not force me into marrying any man unless I wish to do so."

There was silence and she thought her father was going to argue with her. Then he said:

"As I have always been lucky when I follow my hunches, Oletha, I promise you unreservedly!"

"Thank you, Papa."

Oletha's voice was unsteady and she had the feeling that she had not won, as she had intended, a small victory, but had committed herself to the unknown and something which was distinctly frightening.

She had a violent impulse to take back her promise to go to Gore and tell her father she would not meet the Duke and raise his hopes or her father's, since she had no intention of complying with them.

29

Then before she could speak, her father rose from the table to say:

"Come along! We are wasting time and the horses will be waiting for us."

Oletha bit back the words which had already come to her lips.

"Yes, of course, Papa," she agreed. "I will not keep you more than a minute while I get my hat and gloves."

She ran from the room as she spoke and the Colonel, following more slowly, put his hand up to his forehead.

He thought he was a gambler who had bet on a complete outsider, then had found the running better than he had expected.

At the same time, it had not been easy, and he knew as he walked down the corridor that he had been distinctly apprehensive as to how Oletha would react to his suggestions.

Chapter Two

OLETHA PASSED a sleepless night.

She lay in her comfortable bed in the beautiful room that had been specially designed to her own taste, thinking that she was caught in a trap from which she could see very little chance of escape.

She was astute enough to realise that once she went with her father to stay with the Duke and he proposed marriage, it would be almost impossible for her to refuse him.

She was well aware that her father had always longed for greater social recognition than he received in the County of Worcestershire.

It had, in fact, irked him that he and her mother, while acknowledged as well known and respected people, had no precedence compared with the noble families with which the County abounded.

The Earl of Coventry was known over the length and breadth of England and everybody in Worcestershire admired him as a sportsman and a great gentleman.

There were other noblemen such as Lord Cavendish Bentick, brother of the Duke of Portland, and Master of a pack of fox hounds; Lord Dudley living in one of the largest houses in England; Earl Beauchamp in one of the oldest.

It had never occurred to her mother, being American, to mind if she was not seated on her host's right or left at a dinner-party, but from things her father had said from time to time, Oletha knew that he resented not being able to arm into dinner his hostess or one of the more important lady guests.

It seemed trivial compared to the happiness he and her mother enjoyed together, and yet she knew that now her mother was dead and she was heiress to her grandfather's enormous fortune, her father's ambitions for her had increased year by year.

Now she began to understand why he had insisted on her having a very extensive education and why he had been planning for over two years the "splash" she would make in London when she was a debutante.

Because it was considered correct for girls not to be seen or heard until they made their debut,

32

Colonel Ashurst had never allowed Oletha to attend the more important race-meetings or appear at any parties that were not entirely for girls of her own age.

She therefore had very little idea of what social life was like.

When her father and mother entertained she would peep at the dinner-guests when they arrived and watch them in the Dining-Hall from the ancient Minstrels' Gallery which had a carved oak screen in front of it.

She could imagine however that the house-party to which the Duke had invited her would be a very formal one.

With the exception of her father and herself the guests would all be social figures whom the last Duke had entertained and would perhaps even include the Prince and Princess of Wales.

This would mean that the question would obviously be asked why Colonel Ashurst and his daughter had been invited, and it would not require much intelligence to guess the answer.

Oletha could imagine in the circumstances how the Duke would inevitably be humiliated if she refused his proposal of marriage, while her father, whatever he might say to the contrary, would be furiously angry.

"I cannot go to Gore," she told herself. "I have to find some way to refuse now, before it is too late."

She lay thinking of all the possibilities: to say

that she was ill was the first idea which came to her mind.

But she had the feeling that unless she was almost dying, her father would drag her there willy-nilly.

She did not see any other way out, unless she deliberately broke a leg or gave herself concussion by falling off her horse.

"What can I do? What can I do?" she asked into the darkness and even after she had slept a little, she awoke to find the question still ringing in her ears.

She knew by the way her father came downstairs to breakfast that he was in a good humour, having accepted the Duke's invitation and looking forward to the future.

Fortunately the previous night they had had several neighbours to dinner so there had been no chance of private conversation.

Now when they had talked about the weather and had a made a few desultory remarks to each other, Colonel Ashurst said:

"You have not forgotten, Oletha, that I am leaving you this afternoon?"

"I had as a matter of fact, Papa."

"I promised to stay with Lord Ludlow and advise him about some horses he has recently purchased and which he intends to put into training."

"You will enjoy that, Papa," Oletha said automatically.

"Horses always interest me," Colonel Ashurst admitted, "and I intend to go from the Ludlows to London because there is a sale at Tattersall's."

"Is it a big sale, Papa?"

"Not very," the Colonel answered, "but there is a stallion which I consider worth almost any price I may have to pay for it."

"Let me come with you."

Colonel Ashurst shook his head.

"Not on this visit," he replied. "I have been asked to a Regimental dinner which means I should have to leave you alone, and there is also a dinner-party being given by my old friends the Cunninghams."

Oletha gave a little sigh.

"I see I must stay at home like Cinderella."

"I am afraid so, my darling. At the same time, you will have plenty to occupy you with the new studies I have arranged with that Italian Tutor."

"Yes, of course," Oletha agreed. "But I am beginning to feel as if I am stuffed with knowledge like a liver pâté, but with no practical experience of anything but books!"

Her father laughed.

"There is plenty of time for practical experience, as you call it, and that will start when you go to stay with the Duke. Remember I am taking you as a grown up young lady, not as a girl who is still in the School-Room."

"In which case I shall need some more gowns."

"There speaks the eternal woman," her father smiled, "and I have already thought of it."

"You have?"

"Yes, indeed. In fact, I have written to the shop in Hanover Square which your mother always patronised, telling them to have at least a dozen of their most elegant and beautiful creations ready for me to bring back to you when I leave London."

"That sounds delightful, Papa," Oletha said, "but I would have liked to choose them myself."

"You have always approved of my taste in the past," her father said quickly.

"Which has been impeccable," Oletha admitted. "But if I am to be grown up, I would like to try out my own ideas, or at least have a say in what I am to wear."

"Of course, of course!" Colonel Ashurst agreed, "but as time is so short, you will have to leave that for another time. But I will tell you what you can do: if you have any definite ideas as to colour and style for your gowns, write today and tell them what you require. You could even make sketches. After all, you draw well."

"You are very practical, Papa, and that is exactly what I will do," Oletha answered.

Her father glanced at her, realising that she was a little piqued by his high-handed methods and after a moment, he said beguilingly:

"Forgive me, Oletha, if I am rushing you over this, but there is so little time and I have every intention of your being a stupendous, sensational success."

"If you intend me to shine like a star," Oletha said, "I think at least I should be allowed a spotlight and a roll of drums when I appear."

She spoke sarcastically, but she thought cynically that her money would illuminate her far more effectively than any spotlight, and the theme in the mind of everybody who looked at her would be "money—money—money!"

Even to think such a thing was slightly vulgar, but it was inevitable after what her father had said to her last night.

When breakfast was over they rode together as they always did, galloping their horses across the Park, then taking them over the jumps that had been constructed in the paddock.

Watching Oletha take her fences the Colonel thought that no man could fail to appreciate how elegant she looked on a horse, besides having an expertise that was outstanding.

'The Duke will be inhuman if he does not fall in love with her as soon as he sees her,' he thought.

Then he knew that he was still uncertain of Oletha, however complacent she appeared on the surface.

They were too close to each other for him not to be aware of the depth of her feelings that were unusual in so young a girl.

He knew now that she was disturbed by what

he had suggested and although she had not said so, he felt worried.

Because he was anxious for the success of his plans he told himself it was a pity that he was going away just at this particular moment.

Then he changed his mind and decided that perhaps it was a good thing.

He did not wish to talk too much about the Duke or what was waiting for Oletha when she reached Gore.

It would be much better for her to be surprised by the magnificence of it and, Colonel Ashurst hoped, by the appearance of the Duke.

He himself was tremendously impressed by him, but women were unpredictable and Oletha was a woman, although so far a very inexperienced one.

Her horse took the last jump and as she cantered up to him she was smiling.

"Jupiter is getting better every day," she said. "I hope you are pleased with the way I have trained him."

"Delighted!" Colonel Ashurst replied, "and now I think we ought to ride home as I have ordered an early luncheon."

He left as soon as the meal was finished and, feeling somehow lonely which was an unusual sensation, Oletha walked towards the Library.

She had not bothered to tell her father that the Italian Tutor, who had occupied a great deal of her time recently, had sent a message to say he was indisposed with a bad cold and would therefore not be giving her a lesson that afternoon.

"What shall I do with myself?" she wondered.

She knew that because her thoughts were occupied almost exclusively with what was to happen in two weeks time, she felt indecisive.

She looked at the Library which her father had added to and improved since he had been preoccupied with her education, and thought it was a very charming room.

The books which had been added recently occupied one side of it and on the other were the volumes from the original Library, accumulated over the centuries.

Despite the fact that most of the Ashursts had been sportsmen and a great many soldiers, they had also appreciated literature.

It was Oletha who had suggested that many of these books needed repairing, and also that they should be catalogued.

"I have a feeling, Papa," she said, "that some of them are very rare and that means they are also valuable. I think it important we should know exactly what we possess."

Her father had been interested in her suggestion.

"Of course we should have them catalogued," he agreed. "I cannot imagine why I did not think of it myself."

He had written off to the British Museum and they had sent him the names of several experts whom they recommended. Two months ago Mr. Baron had started work in the Library.

Oletha had been delighted to find she had been right, and quite a number of the books were highly valued by mediaeval scholars, and others were of great interest to historians.

Some were in very bad condition and these Mr. Baron had sent to be repaired, saying that it was something which should have been done years ago.

"You must not complain," Oletha laughed, "they might have remained as they were for at least another century if I had not told Papa that something should be done about them."

"Future Ashursts and posterity will be grateful to you," Mr. Baron replied.

Now, looking at the order in which he had arranged the books on the shelves, Oletha picked out one which was a beautifully illustrated 15th-century manual.

She was turning over the pages when the door of the Library opened and Mr. Baron came into the room.

Oletha smiled at him and said:

"I was thinking how neatly you have arranged everything."

"Thank you, Miss Ashurst," Mr. Baron replied. "I have just heard that your father has left."

"Yes. He has gone away for a few days."

"Then I owe him an apology."

"What for?" Oletha asked.

"As no-one told me he would not be here, I omitted to inform him that I must leave tomorrow."

"Tomorrow!" Oletha exclaimed.

"My work here is finished," Mr. Baron replied. "In fact I have here the complete catalogue that I had intended to present to your father this afternoon."

He held out the book as he spoke and Oletha saw that, in alphabetical order, he had set down in his elegant copper-plate writing all the books, listing each one with the author, its date and in many cases, a short description of its contents.

"It is really finished?" she asked. "How wonderful! I know my father will be delighted!"

"I hope he will be," Mr. Baron said, "and I only wish I had realised this morning that he was leaving. I could have told him how much I have enjoyed my work here and thanked him for his kindness to me."

"I will tell my father what you have said," Oletha replied, "and I know when he has seen this catalogue he will write and thank you himself."

"I should appreciate that very much," Mr. Baron answered. "I think it will interest you, Miss Ashurst, seeing that it was you who realised the rarity and the value of so many of the volumes."

"I know much more about them now," Oletha smiled, "and I should really be thanking you for all you have taught me."

"It has been a very great pleasure," Mr. Baron said courteously.

"Why are you in such a hurry to leave?" Oletha asked turning the pages of the catalogue. "After all, Papa will be back in under a week, and I know how he would like to talk to you about this himself."

"The fact is, Miss Ashurst," Mr. Baron replied, "I have had a letter today asking me to catalogue a Library in which I believe I shall find perhaps even more undiscovered treasures than there are here."

The way he spoke made Oletha look up at him curiously and she remarked:

"You sound quite excited about it."

Mr. Baron laughed.

"That is true, Miss Ashurst, I am! In my work, which is so often spent rather drearily cataloguing Public Libraries from which the volumes have been stolen or defaced, it is only occasionally I get the chance of coming to a private house where there is a great wealth of books, often unappreciated and unknown."

"I quite see it must be fun for you," Oletha said, "and where is the Library to which you are going now?"

"It is the Library at Gore, Miss Ashurst, and I understand from the letter I have received from the Duke's secretary, that although there are thousands of books there, they have in fact, never been listed."

"Gore!" Oletha murmured beneath her breath.

"It is one of the finest houses in England," Mr. Baron said, "and I have always heard of the Library but never had a change of visiting it. Who knows, since the Dukes of Gorleston come from a family which has played a part in the history of this country, there may be manuscripts and folios of inestimable value hidden away there."

The enthusiasm in his voice was infectious, but Oletha was thinking not of books, but of herself.

It seemed an extraordinary coincidence, almost as if it was fate, that Mr. Baron should be going to Gore just at this particular moment when the Duke had come into her life in a very unexpected manner.

Hardly aware of what she was doing, she put the book she had been looking at back in its place on the shelf, and as she did so, Mr. Baron said:

"I thought you would appreciate that manual, Miss Ashurst, and I have not forgotten that you drew my attention to Plutarch's *Vitae Illustrium Viriorum*, which I might have missed if you had not pointed it out to me."

He laughed.

"If the time ever comes when you have to earn your own living, I am sure there is a career waiting for you as a Curator."

He was surprised when Oletha looked at him in a startled fashion.

Then she said:

"I want to talk to you, Mr. Baron. Will you come and sit down on the window-seat? I need your . . . help."

The following morning, driving in her father's comfortable carriage towards the Railway Station, Oletha told herself she was setting out on an adventure that might almost have been the subject of one of the books in the Library.

She had planned every detail of it after she had talked to Mr. Baron yesterday, and had lain awake during the night going over and over every point one by one, in case she missed anything that might betray her.

Strangely enough, like a puzzle falling into place, everything seemed to grow clearer and clearer instead of becoming more difficult.

The first hurdle had been, of course, to persuade Mr. Baron that what she intended to do with his help was not only feasible but right and proper from her point of view.

At first he had been shocked at the very idea and said firmly that he could not take part in any plan which involved deceiving either her father or the Duke.

Then as she confided in him, urged him, and finally beseeched him, he had given way.

She did not realise that in trying to persuade him, she looked so lovely, and yet in a way so

44

pathetic, that any man, whatever his age, would have found her irresistible.

"I am sure I am doing the wrong thing, Miss Ashurst," Mr. Baron said at last. "In fact, you are asking me to put at risk and perhaps destroy what has hitherto been a blameless career."

"I promise you shall not suffer on my account," Oletha said, "and all I am asking you to do, is not to go to Gore for four days. You will send a telegram to the Duke saying that you are on your way."

She paused, then continued:

"When I arrive I will explain that at the last moment you were unavoidably detained and that as I am your assistant and always work with you, I have come temporarily in your place."

"Surely they will think as you are so young, that it is a little strange?" Mr. Baron protested uncomfortably.

"Then I will say I am your daughter. No-one could possibly object to that relationship."

"No, indeed, but you must understand, Miss Ashurst, that it would be very unlikely for me to have a daughter who looked like you."

Oletha smiled.

"Who is to think that without seeing you?" she asked. "Besides, you are being over-modest, Mr. Baron. I can think of no possible reason why your daughter, if you had one, should not be very attractive and certainly very clever."

It took Oletha nearly two hours to persuade

45

him, but finally he succumbed and agreed to stay on at the Manor for another four days until finally he journeyed to Gore.

"As soon as you arrive, I can leave," Oletha said. "I will return here before Papa gets back from London and I shall have learnt all I want to know about the Duke."

"When he realises who you are, Miss Ashurst, what will he say to me?"

"That is quite easy," Oletha answered. "I shall tell him you knew nothing about it. You can say you thought you had finished here, then found there was a whole lot of books you had omitted to catalogue, and because you felt you owed your loyalty to Papa as he engaged you first, you decided you must finish up here before you took on another job."

The plan sounded plausible even to Oletha and it was obvious that although he tried, Mr. Baron could find no flaw in it.

Then there was the difficulty of persuading her father's secretary that she should go away.

"The Colonel said nothing about your leaving, Miss Ashurst," Mr. Allen protested.

"I only opened the letter from my friend, inviting me to stay, after Papa had left," Oletha replied. "As he was worried about leaving me alone, I know he will be delighted that I can go to Elizabeth Grayson's."

At the name Mr. Allen's look of anxiety vanished.

"If you are going to stay with Lady Grayson,

46

I am sure it would be quite all right, Miss Oletha, but you did not mention that at first."

"I will travel by train to Paddington and they will meet me there," Oletha said.

Mr. Allen made no more objections and it was only her old maid who grumbled at having to pack up everything so quickly.

Martha was always the same. If she was given plenty of time she took journeys, wherever they might be, in her stride, but she disliked being hurried.

"I will need very little," Oletha said, "because Papa is buying me a whole lot of new clothes and I am tired of these anyway."

"I've never heard such extravagance!" Martha said with the familiarity of an old retainer. "You've not had more than a few months wear out of the last selection of gowns anyway."

"I know that," Oletha said, "but they are too young for me, and I intend to wear something quite different now that I am grown up."

Martha was not listening, but she was merely filling the trunk and grumbling as she did so.

Oletha was concentrating on planning how she could be rid of her and knew this was going to be extremely difficult.

She could hardly as a Curator's daughter arrive with a lady's-maid. At the same time, it would be unthinkable for her to travel alone even a short distance, and certainly not if going to stay with her friend.

She thought it over very carefully and knew

that the one thing she must not do would be to dispense with Martha before she left home.

She was quite certain that if Mr. Allen thought there was anything strange about her journey he would immediately telegraph to her father.

Though she tossed and turned all night, Oletha had found no solution to this problem by the time morning came.

One possible chance was, she thought, to take Martha into her confidence. But she knew that would be a mistake and she had the feeling that the old maid who was no actress would undoubtedly give her away when they reached Gore.

It was only when they had actually set off in the train and were travelling in a reserved carriage having been seen off by Mr. Allen and their luggage deposited in the Guard's Van by a footman that Oletha had an inspiration.

She moved from her seat to sit next to Martha on the other side of the carriage.

"I think I told you, Martha," she said, "that I had a letter from Nanny about a month ago."

"Yes, you told me, Miss Oletha," Martha replied.

"You remember Nanny said that she was hoping we would visit her when we were next in London?"

"I remembers that too," Martha agreed.

"What I am going to ask you to do is to go and stay with Nanny for the next four days."

"Why should I be doing that, Miss Oletha?" Martha enquired in astonishment.

48

"Because I did not like to tell you before we left home, but Lady Grayson asked me particularly not to bring a lady's-maid."

"Why should she do that?" Martha enquired indignantly. "I've been there often enough before."

"Yes, I know," Oletha agreed, "but you know the house is not very big and apparently Miss Elizabeth has quite a large party. Sir Robert and Lady Grayson have some of their own friends there as well. That means every room is full."

"Then why didn't you tell me?" Martha enquired, and there was still an indignant note in her voice.

"Because, Martha dear," Oletha replied, "you know what a fuss-pot Mr. Allen is, especially when Papa is away from home. He would never have allowed me to travel alone to London, but would have come himself, and you know what a bore he is."

She put her hand over that of the old maid.

"I always enjoy going anywhere with you, Martha, and three hours in the train in the company of Mr. Allen and three hours back, would have sent me nearly crazy!"

She saw that Martha look gratified and went on:

"Besides, in asking you to go to Nanny I am being selfish. I have a whole list of things I want you to buy for me in London, before we go to stay with the Duke."

She knew, because nothing could ever be kept

49

from the servants, that everybody at home would know by this time that she and her father had been invited to Gore.

Her father's valet would doubtless have told Martha how smart she must be, especially if the Prince of Wales was likely to be present.

"Papa says he is buying me a lot of new gowns," Oletha went on, "but you know as well as I do that he will forget about the accessories. Men always do."

"That's true enough," Martha conceded. "But you should be choosing such things yourself."

"You know exactly what I like," Oletha replied, "and I want to go to Elizabeth's party. It is sure to be fun."

She knew she was getting her own way.

"Now help me, Martha, to make a list of all the things I shall want if I am to look dazzling as Papa insists when we stay with the Duke."

This was entirely in Martha's province and she rattled off a whole list of accessories while Oletha wrote them down.

When she had filled several closely written pages torn from the back of her small diary, she thought with satisfaction that with any luck Martha would be too busy shopping to have time to call at their own house in London and gossip with the servants.

But she took the precaution to say aloud:

"I think it would be better if you did not go to Park Lane. If Papa knows I am staying away without you, he is sure to make a fuss."

"If you don't think your father would approve, Miss Oletha, you've no right to go. I can't think why Her Ladyship invited you in such a half-hearted manner."

"She was very apologetic," Oletha replied, "but you know as well as I do, you would hate to be squeezed into a room with somebody else's maid."

She remembered how much Martha had grumbled when this had happened sometimes in the past, and after a minute the old maid said:

"Well, I dare say you'll come to no harm, and you'll certainly need everything on that list when you are staying at Gore."

"Then please buy them for me," Oletha said, "and anything else you see that I should like to have."

Martha put the list away in her large black leather handbag and Oletha went back to her own seat with a feeling of triumph.

She had been clever, very clever, she told herself, and she felt she had been cleverer still when on reaching Paddington she managed by hailing the first empty cab that was waiting outside the station to send Martha away before she left herself.

"I must wait to see you into Her Ladyship's carriage, Miss Oletha," Martha protested.

Oletha had banked on her being agitated and a little bewildered as she always was at stations.

"I can see them waiting for me up the road," she said, "so get in while you have the chance, Martha, otherwise you may have to wait ages for another cab."

"But, Miss Oletha . . .!" Martha protested.

"I am all right. I am going to join Miss Elizabeth now," Oletha replied, and walked away followed by the porter who carried her luggage on a truck.

She waited until the carriage which carried Martha was out of sight, then said to the man:

"I want to take a train to Beaconsfield. I think there is one in about half-an-hour."

"That's right, Miss—at twelve-twenty-three."

"Thank you," Oletha said. "Will you take me to the right platform?"

When the porter had found her a seat in the First Class carriage, he accepted with a look of surprise the very large tip she gave him and Oletha sat back with a feeling of satisfaction and achievement.

It was the first time in her life she had ever travelled except in a reserved carriage and without being seen off by either one of her father's secretaries or the Butler. She had certainly never done anything so wild or so reprehensible as to lie, as she had done in the last twenty-four hours, to those who were in charge of her.

"I have escaped, and for the moment no-one has any idea where I am," Oletha said, beneath her breath.

She told herself it must be her American blood which enabled her to behave in such an outrageous manner.

She was quite certain that her friends, as well as her father, would be horrified at what she intended to do, but she knew that when it was a case of self-preservation only desperate measures would suffice.

'I shall see what the Duke is really like without his being aware of me,' she decided.

She might not have a chance to talk to him, but she would see him in his own environment and hear what those he employed thought about him. If he ever did speak to her, he would not put on a 'pretty face' for somebody as insignificant as a Curator's daughter.

She was not quite certain in what rank of society she would come in her assumed position in the household.

She was aware of course, that she would not be invited to dine with the Duke or indeed have any meal with him, but if the way her father had treated Mr. Baron was anything to go by, she would not eat with the servants.

She would be "betwixt and between," like a Governess or a companion or, she supposed, something like her father's secretaries who, both in London and in the country, lived an isolated existence which went with the authority they needed to run the house and her father's estate.

She wondered how she should address the

Duke and decided she must call him "Your Grace" and she supposed she ought to drop him a little curtsy when they first met.

Then it struck her that perhaps she would never meet him. He might not be interested enough in his books to wish to discuss them with a Curator.

Then she told herself that he must be interested, otherwise he would not have sent for Mr. Baron in the first place.

It suddenly struck her why he had done so. He needed money!

It was something that had not occurred to her before, but now it was perfectly obvious that the Duke was perhaps considering selling some of the books to raise the money he needed so badly.

This seemed extremely likely and the only question was whether if he obtained enough from that particular source he would then not feel obliged to marry a rich wife.

Oletha turned a dozen different explanations over in her mind.

There was also, she thought, every chance that the Library, like the rest of his possessions, was in trust, in which case the only reason for having it catalogued would be to assess its value and make sure that nothing in the future was missing.

'I will find out the truth when I arrive,' she thought.

She knew, now she was nearing her destination, that she was not only excited but also rather frightened.

She felt nervously that perhaps the moment she arrived, the Duke would say:

"I know who you are! You are Colonel Ashurst's daughter!"

If he did that nothing could be more humiliating.

Then she knew she was merely letting her imagination run away with her.

Of course there was no likelihood of his doing anything of the sort. He had never seen her and would have no idea what she looked like. Moreover from all her father had said, he had not been particularly curious.

'I suppose it would have been embarrassing for him,' she told herself, 'to say to Papa: "Is your daughter pretty or plain?" Perhaps he would just assume that I am the latter.'

She thought of her friend who complained of her being both rich and beautiful, and told herself the Duke should think himself lucky if she agreed to marry him, as her father wished.

Then she remembered that men had different tastes. Her father had always said that he hated very large women.

"Brunhildas frighten me!" he had declared. "I like women to be small, dainty and graceful, like you and your mother!"

"Then you are out of fashion," her mother protested. "You know as well as I do it is the vogue to be tall and Junoesque."

"Not in my house!" the Colonel had said firmly

55

and her mother had laughed.

Oletha's father had always teased both her and her mother because they had such tiny feet.

"They are very attractive," he said, "but they look too small to support you."

"We manage," Mrs. Ashurst replied, "and I would hate to have feet like the average Englishwoman who always looks as if she does nothing but tramp across fields and up hills."

"You look as if you do nothing but dance on rose-petals," the Colonel had teased, "and then you would never crush them."

They had laughed at his flights of fancy, but Oletha, catching a glimpse of her smart black shoes peeping out from beneath her travelling-gown, thought that her feet might give her away, if nothing else.

She was sure that Mr. Baron's daughter would take a size six, while her fitting was barely three.

She heard the porter call out the name of the station and for a moment did not move.

Instinctively she waited for Martha to collect her things in the carriage and she was expecting there would be a footman to hurry to the Guard's Van.

"I am on my own," she told herself severely, "and the sooner I remember it the better!"

As soon as the train stopped she got out of the carriage quickly.

She had an idea that Mr. Baron's daughter

would have travelled Second Class.

When she had bought her ticket, something she had never done before, the man in the Ticket Office after taking one look at her, had said:

"First Class, Ma'am?" and she had agreed without thinking.

There was nobody waiting on the platform and she walked towards the Guard's Van looking at the passengers who were alighting from the carriages.

Then she saw standing by the exit a footman with a cockaded top-hat on his head and an elaborate crested livery.

She walked up to him.

"Are you by any chance, here to meet Mr. Baron?" she enquired.

"Yes, Ma'am," the footman replied respectfully.

"Then you are from Gore," Oletha said, "and I have come in Mr. Baron's place. He has unfortunately been detained in London, but I am his daughter."

She thought the flunkey looked surprised, but he said after a brief pause:

"The carriage is waiting outside for you, Ma'am, and if you've some luggage in the van I'll tell a porter to find it."

"There are three trunks and a hat box," Oletha replied.

She had been aware that this was rather a lot

of luggage for a Curator's daughter, but it had been difficult enough to prevent Martha from packing even more.

Anyway, she told herself, it was none of the servant's business and they were hardly likely to tell the Duke she was so well equipped.

The footman led the way to where waiting outside the station was a very smart closed carriage drawn by two horses.

Oletha climbed in and there was a short delay before her luggage was brought by the porter. Then the footman jumped up on the box and they were off.

Oletha gave a little sigh of relief.

"So far, so good!"

Whatever anyone might say, she had managed very skilfully to travel alone and get herself to where she wanted to go.

Anyone who had been as cosseted and protected as she had been would understand what an achievement it had been, and in a way, she thought with a smile, it was like reaching the North Pole or climbing to the top of Mount Everest.

Now the really difficult part began and as she leaned back against the comfortable padded seat, she knew that she was tense and, although she hated to admit it, a little frightened.

"The worst thing that can happen is that I am discovered," she told herself. "Then the Duke will send me home in disgrace and say that I am the last woman on earth he wants for his wife."

That would be quite a relief in itself, she thought.

Then she found herself wondering as she had done already a dozen times, if her father had been right when he said no decent Englishman would ever ask her to marry him.

It struck Oletha, not for the first time, that this was a very dismal prospect.

"I am not sure that I want to be married," she told herself, "but I ... want to be ... loved."

Chapter Three

THE DUKE of Gorleston finished signing his letters, then as he pushed aside the last one, his secretary, who had served his father before him, said:

"There is a letter, your Grace, which I think you will find slightly perturbing."

The Duke raised his eyebrows.

He thought that a great many things had been perturbing since he had inherited, and one more would make little difference to the sum total which he found extremely worrying.

"It is almost the duplicate of another letter which came for Your Grace last week," Mr. Hansard went on, "with which I did not trouble you."

"What is it about?" the Duke enquired.

"It is about the Library, Your Grace, and it is from an American who is interested in collecting old books. It seems strange that it should arrive just after you told me you had engaged a Curator."

"What does the letter say?" the Duke enquired.

"He is a private gentleman who says he has heard, which he admits was only a rumour, that there was a likelihood of there being a Shakespeare folio in the Gorleston collection, and if you were thinking of disposing of it privately he would wish to have first refusal."

The Duke stared at his secretary in astonishment.

"A Shakespeare folio!" he exclaimed. "Are you telling me that is a possibility?"

"Personally, I think it is most unlikely, Your Grace, but as there is no catalogue of the contents of the Library, there must be a possibility that it might be there."

"I cannot believe if there was, there would not be some mention of it in my father's papers, or rather my grandfather's."

"I agree with Your Grace," Mr. Hansard answered. "At the same time, I'm sorry the rumour should have reached America."

"Are you telling me that it is something which has been talked about in England?"

"Only in the last month," Mr. Hansard replied.

The Duke frowned before he said:

61

"What is the other letter to which you referred?"

"It came from one of the best-known establishments that deal in antique books in London, and the owner wrote to the same effect that there was a rumour that there might be some valuable books in your collection and that he would like to have first refusal, if they are for sale."

"I agree with you, it is strange to receive two such letters in a short space of time," the Duke said. "Do you suppose that somebody who knows the Library has been talking out of turn, or is it just speculation on the part of two people, one in England and one across the Atlantic?"

"I really do not know, Your Grace, but I am extremely relieved that I have had a telegram to say that Mr. Baron, who is vouched for by the British Museum, will be arriving today."

"Are you suggesting we might be burgled?" the Duke asked incredulously.

"I think that is unlikely," Mr. Hansard replied, "and of course I will ensure that the night-watchmen are made aware that they must keep a close eye on the Library as well as on every other part of the house. At the same time, the whole thing makes me a trifle anxious."

"Anxious?" the Duke repeated.

He felt Mr. Hansard had something else to say but was a little embarrassed. Then as if he felt it was his duty to speak, he said:

"As a matter of fact, Captain Harry asked me

today if he could have the key to the Library."

"The key?"

"Until Mr. Baron arrives I thought, Your Grace, considering the two letters we have received, that it would be a good idea to keep the Library locked unless you wish yourself to use the room."

"And Captain Harry wished to enter the Library ?"

"Yes, Your Grace."

Mr. Hansard quickly picked up the papers and letters that the Duke had signed and seemed in a hurry to leave the room.

The Duke did not detain him and when his secretary was gone he sat at his desk with a frown between his eyes.

He was well aware that Mr. Hansard, who had been with his father for twenty-five years, would not have spoken unless he was really worried by Harry's request.

Quite frankly the Duke was not surprised.

Ever since he had returned home from India, Harry Goring, a cousin who was also his heir presumptive, had been worrying him for a loan or preferably a gift of money, which the Duke, in fact, could not possibly afford to give him.

At first Harry's request had been jovial.

"I am sure you will understand, old Man, that as your father was ill, I did not like to worry him before he died."

When this evoked no response, he became

more insistent, more demanding.

The Duke was an extremely astute judge of men, and when he saw his cousin after seven years, he knew that he disliked him as much, if not more, than he had when they had been boys together.

Harry Goring was a hanger-on of the rich, the type of man who had never done a day's work in his life, and had no intention of doing anything but enjoy himself.

He had been put in a County Regiment by his father and had reached the rank, for a short while, of acting Captain. Contrary to regular precedent, he had continued to use his temporary rank after he left the Regiment.

It was the sort of thing that made him very unpopular except with the type of women who found him good-looking and amusing and enjoyed his somewhat over-effusive compliments.

The Duke, as soon as he understood the financial situation at Gore, had made it very clear to his cousin that he had no spare funds to give or lend to impecunious relations.

"Dammit all!" Harry had exclaimed, "you are now the head of the family and you are supposed to look after us."

"I am well aware of my responsibilities," the Duke answered coldly, "but one cannot squeeze blood from a stone, and I can only point out, Harry that you are young and healthy while there are a number of elderly relatives who are more in need than you are ever likely to be."

"But I am your heir presumptive," Harry said aggressively.

The Duke's lips had twisted in a wry smile.

"I am not yet senile," he said, "and there is every possibility of my marrying and having a son, so I should not count on borrowing on the chance of stepping into my shoes."

He knew by the expression on his cousin's face that he had already thought of the second possibility, and he said sharply:

"I am being quite frank with you, Harry, when I say that I cannot afford to pay your debts nor bail you out now or in the immediate future. The pensioners and the servants whom I have had to retire must come first. The family will have to wait a considerable time before I am in a position to help any of them."

"You can surely sell something."

The Duke gave a little laugh, but it was not one of amusement.

"I have thought of that already, but everything is entailed."

He thought when he spoke that it was the truth, and it was only a month later when he was going through the insurances that he found that the Library was listed at £1,000.

"Surely that is very low?" he had asked Mr. Hansard.

"I have often thought so myself, Your Grace," was the reply, "but your father protested every year when the question of insurance was raised, and as there is no catalogue it is impossible to know whether anything in the Library is of value."

"No catalogue!" the Duke exclaimed. "But surely that is extraordinary?"

"If there ever was one, it has been lost," Mr. Hansard answered. "So quite frankly, Your Grace, the Library is an unknown quantity. But there must surely be some first editions which have become valuable over the years. I am not an expert and your father was only interested in contemporary biographies and books on sport."

"I remember how much he enjoyed those," the Duke remarked.

Then in a more serious tone he said:

"What you are telling me is that the contents of the Library are not in trust."

"They are not, Your Grace."

The Duke digested this information slowly before he said:

"I think the first thing to do is to have a catalogue made of everything it contains. We must find a Curator who is trustworthy."

"I will write to the British Museum, Your Grace. I am sure they will be only too willing to send us a reliable man when they know it is for the Library at Gore."

The Duke agreed that a letter should be dispatched immediately.

The more he thought about it the more it seemed extraordinary to him that a Library that was so magnificent and so well-known should never have been properly catalogued.

He was well aware that its real fame lay in the fact that the room had been specially designed by Robert Adam when he had completely renovated the house that had existed on the same site since the reign of Queen Elizabeth.

Adam's design for the Library, which was the finest he had ever executed, had been copied by other great houses and was illustrated in almost every book which described the architectural masterpieces of Great Britain.

Apparently however, few people had been concerned with its contents, and it seemed to the Duke that perhaps here was an answer to his immediate problems: he might be able to sell some of the more valuable books.

At the same time, he knew it was something he was loath to do, because he felt that morally he was obliged to keep all the treasures of Gore intact for the future generations who would follow after him.

At the same time, his position was almost intolerable.

Because he had never expected to inherit, he had not, when he was at home, troubled to ascertain what were the expenses of his father's racing stable, let alone his vast estates with their various departments, which made the whole thing, as someone had once said: "A state within a state."

There was the house itself, which the Duke now realised gobbled up money like a fire-breathing dragon, and there were also all the accessories to it, the dairies, the laundry, the workshops for carpenters and stone-masons.

All these required a large amount of people to run them, and the game-keepers, the foresters, and the gardeners were also needed, besides a large household staff.

When the Duke had seen the number of people who were employed he thought that he had, to all intents and purposes, a private army of his own, but unfortunately there was no benign tax-payer to enable him to afford them.

Then he realised that the majority of those who worked at Gore considered themselves part of the family, and if they were turned away they would not only be bewildered and bereft, but would have little chance of finding similar employment elsewhere.

"What can I do? What the devil can I do?" the Duke asked himself.

Night after night he sat in his Study and added up the enormous amount of money that was required not only for debts which had been left unpaid for far too long, but for the ordinary everyday upkeep of his possessions.

It was because he had learned never to act

hastily but always to consider things from every angle before taking action, that when he first arrived he had let things continue as they were, while he investigated very thoroughly the whole structure of which he was now the head.

The Duke had always been a reserved man owing to the fact that he had been sent to a boarding school at a very early age, and being unusually intelligent he found himself, when he reached Eton, in a class of boys who were all older than he was.

He had therefore learned to keep quiet and not assert himself, so that the habit of self-control and what the servants called: "keeping himself to himself" had remained with him when he went into the Regiment.

Because his father was a Duke it had stood him in good stead that he was so quiet and unpretentious.

Older people thought him modest and unassuming, and his contemporaries, finding that he put on "no airs," liked him for himself.

When he became the youngest Major of the British Army in India, and the last year before his father died the youngest acting Colonel, the congratulations he received were whole-hearted and without envy.

"A damned fine soldier!" the hard-bitten veterans said to each other, while his brother-officers were genuinely pleased with his success, because they both admired and trusted him.

"One can rely on Goring," they said to each other. "He would never let you down, and I would rather be with him in a tight spot than with anybody else I know."

There were quite a number of "tight spots" on the North-West Frontier in which Sandor Goring had distinguished himself, and for which he was mentioned in despatches twice in the same year.

But just as he was looking forward to being gazetted as Colonel, he learned that his father had died and he had to return home immediately.

It was not such a shock as it would have been twelve months earlier when he knew that on the death of his brother he was heir to the Dukedom.

But he had, in fact, been confident that his father would live for at least another ten or fifteen years, and he had therefore given little thought to the difference his brother's death would make in his own life.

Now he was faced with a campaign that was just as difficult as those in which he had fought successfully in India, only this time the enemy was not the tribesmen, but money, and far more elusive.

The Duke however confided in no-one.

He talked with his father's Solicitors and relied on Mr. Hansard for details which only he knew.

He did not tell even them what he intended to do, and the only outsider whom he turned to in his difficulties was his father's friend who he was well aware was acknowledged as the greatest expert on race-horses in the country—Colonel Ashurst.

The Colonel's suggestion that he should solve his problems by taking a rich wife had come as a shock.

If he had fired a cannon at him at close-quarters the Duke could not have been more astonished.

Because he was extremely attractive and a very masculine man, women had, of course, played a part in his life, but actually a very small part.

That he was attracted by them and they by him was inevitable, and he had enjoyed the interludes that took place when he was on leave at Simla or at other hill stations, in the same manner that a man might enjoy the fragrance and beauty of flowers, then forget them as soon as they faded.

It was doubtful if the memory of any particular woman remained long in his mind after he had rejoined his Regiment.

When they wrote to him passionate letters on writing-paper which carried their own particular fragrance, Sandor Goring would often have difficulty in remembering the episodes to which they referred so yearningly.

He found it difficult to be sympathetic with some of the young Subalterns who, returning from leave, wandered about with vacant expressions in their eyes and found it difficult to take up their Regimental duties with any enthusiasm.

As far as women were concerned, like Napoleon, the Duke shut them away in the cupboards of his mind, and did not even think of them as he became immersed in the dangers and intrigues which were an indivisible part of his life as a soldier.

He had always promised himself that when he had time, he would marry and have a family.

He was well aware that his ancestry was something to be proud of. There had been Gorings who had altered the history of England, and down the ages all of them had served their country in one capacity or another, the majority as Statesmen or as soldiers and sailors.

They had been in every Monarch's court, every famous battle, every Naval victory.

He knew he must have a son to follow in his footsteps and become the 6th Duke of Gorleston.

The Dukedom was a fairly recent creation, but the Earldom and the Baroncy went back to the first Goring who had been rewarded by Queen Elizabeth for his courage against the Spaniards.

The idea in principle of a wife and children that would be his in the future was quite different from contemplating marriage with a woman whose only attraction was that she had money.

The Duke was well aware that there was something in what Colonel Ashurst said, and what his ancestors had considered essential was the continuance of the family and its wealth.

There was one Goring who had married an

heiress from the North who owned a great deal of property in Liverpool.

She had certainly not had blue blood, and her portrait showed a homely face with a plebeian nose and rather small eyes.

A century later there was an heiress who came from the West Country whose father had made a fortune in the slave trade.

There was no doubt that she had been delighted to be a Duchess, and there were no less than four portraits of her on the walls at Gore showing her to have a pretty, if rather foolish face, and undoubtedly an exaggerated idea of her own attractions.

There were others, fat, thin, with heavy jaws and low foreheads, women who had brought gold into the family coffers, added broad acres to the estates, and borne sons to carry on the name of Goring.

Their dash and valour however, had come from the paternal side of their breeding rather than the maternal.

The Duke had walked around the rooms of the great house looking at the portraits of his ancestors, knowing that if they could speak they would tell him that it was his duty to follow in their footsteps to save the house and the estates and ignore his own irrelevant feelings.

But he knew the idea of marrying simply for money disgusted him and made him feel cheap.

His own father and mother had, he always believed, married because they were in love.

Now when he thought about it, although his mother was not an heiress, she was a daughter of the Duke of Hull, and he suspected because it was such a suitable match, that the marriage had been arranged.

"Blue blood to blue blood, that is what I always say," had been one of the old Duke's favourite phrases. "Whether it concerns a horse or a woman, one should always breed from the best."

Sandor must unconsciously have imbibed such sentiments from the time he was a small boy. But when he thought of marriage he always imagined his wife would be as lovely and sensitive as his mother had been.

The fourth Duchess had been acclaimed a beauty, especially after her husband inherited. But she also had character and a sympathy and understanding which made her loved by everybody with whom she came in contact.

She was very friendly, very compassionate, without in any way losing her dignity or letting anyone take advantage of her sweetness.

When she had died everybody on the estate had mourned her besides her friends who seemed to range over the whole country.

Her son remembered hearing people say over and over again: "She was a great lady!"

That is what he always expected his wife

would be, and he told himself it would be impossible for a woman who was half American to take his mother's place.

He knew enough about the Ashursts to realise that the Colonel was a gentleman in the real sense of the word, but he knew nothing about his wife, except that he had been told she had been immensely rich and was American born.

"I will not put somebody who does not know how to behave at the head of my table," the Duke vowed to himself as he walked to the end of the Picture Gallery.

Then he asked what was the alternative?

Miss Ashurst was certainly not the only heiress in England and he was well aware that a Ducal coronet was what every socialite yearned to possess, and London would undoubtedly welcome him with open arms.

But it was all a question of time, and the more he looked at the accounts the more he understood that the sands were running out and he had to come to a decision quickly.

His first impulse, as he had told Colonel Ashurst, was to sell his father's racing-stable.

The old Duke had been moderately successful as an owner, but the expenses he had incurred were astronomical.

Although the new Duke had allowed the horses already entered for Goodwood and Doncaster to race, he had known that it would be impossible for him to carry on another season and it was not just a question of making the stringest economies but dispensing with the whole stable.

The same applied to the shoot that had been planned before his father's death to take place in two week's time.

The guests had been invited and were more or less the same who came every year, and he was still waiting to hear whether the Prince of Wales would be one of them.

"His Royal Highness has invariably attended the first shoot at Gore," Mr. Hansard said, "but I have been in touch with his Comptroller and he is not certain whether other arrangements were made immediately the Prince learned of your father's death."

"You mean the Prince was uncertain if I would carry on my father's traditions and His Royal Highness did not wish to miss a day's shooting?"

There was a touch of sarcasm in the Duke's voice and Mr. Hansard replied a little hesitatingly:

"Naturally everybody with a big shoot is only too anxious to entertain His Royal Highness."

"Of course," the Duke agreed, "so I feel we must not disappoint him."

"As a matter of fact," Mr. Hansard replied, "I am quite certain, Your Grace, that His Royal Highness is anxious to come to Gore, and his Comptroller is only keeping me on tenterhooks, so to speak."

The Duke laughed.

"I thought it was I in that position!"

Before Mr. Hansard could reply, he added:

"I hope he comes. It may be for the last time."

His secretary started.

"Are you saying, Your Grace, that you may not have a shoot next year?"

"I am not saying that," the Duke answered, "for I enjoy shooting, I always have. But it is doubtful, Hansard, if we can afford to put down pheasants or entertain on the scale that we are doing on this occasion."

Mr. Hansard sighed.

"To be invited to Gore for one of the shooting-parties," he said, is the ambition of every good game-shot in the country."

"I am sure it is," the Duke said dryly, "but I doubt if many of them have any idea of what it costs."

Now he asked himself how many other things would have to be given up.

Inevitably his mind went to those who were employed, and he felt that if he had to dismiss them it would be almost like turning out of the Regiment men who had followed him into danger and been proud to do so.

He found himself looking at the picture of the Goring who had been Courtier to Charles II, and there came into his mind the famous words of Henry of Navarre:

"Paris is well worth a Mass."

To adapt the words to his own situation he told himself it should be: "Gore is well worth a marriage," and that his own personal feelings in the matter were of very little consequence.

'This is my Kingdom,' he thought as he went to the window.

He stood looking out at the lake, and the trees in the Park which had stood for hundreds of years.

"My kingdom," he repeated beneath his breath, "and as such, I have to defend it and if necessary sacrifice my life to it."

It was then he had gone back to his Study to write to Colonel Ashurst and invite him and his daughter to come and stay for the first shoot in two week's time.

He wondered what other possibilities there were and if there might be a chance to save Gore in other ways.

He made enquiries as to what mineral possibilities there were on the estate, knowing that many of those who would sit with him in the House of Lords had found seams of coal under their green fields.

But Gore in Buckinghamshire was predominately agricultural on chalk soil, and there was no evidence or even any possibility that underneath there lay any valuable minerals.

This brought his mind back to the Library.

He found himself wondering why Harry had asked for the key.

He was quite certain that his cousin seldom, if ever, read a book unless it was the latest Biography which had excited the fashionable gossips.

It made him suspect that Harry must have heard the rumours of there being something valuable in the Library of which nobody in the house had any prior knowledge.

He had hoped that his cousin, after failing for the second time to extract money from him, would have gone home, but he had settled down at Gore and the Duke was reluctant to tell him that he preferred his absence to his company.

It was difficult to be disagreeable or indeed ungenerous to the man who would be his successor should he fall dead or fail to produce a son of his own.

As the Duke had the uncomfortable feeling that his cousin was both envying and resenting him, he had no wish to make things worse by being unpleasant.

Other members of his family had invited themselves to Gore not because, the Duke knew, they had any particular affection for him, but because they were curious to see what he was like after being abroad for so many years.

He had entertained them one after another, and when Harry arrived, he already had two elderly aunts and an ancient cousin crippled with arthritis staying with him and he found his cousin's presence almost a welcome relief.

Because Harry was almost a professional as an entertaining guest, he had made his relatives laugh at his jokes, and paid them compliments in his own rather obvious manner which charmed them into thinking he was very much better than his reputation suggested.

When they had gone he said frankly to the Duke:

"My God, Sandor, we have some ghastly relations! I warn you, if you let them, they will move into Gore and you will have the greatest difficulty in ever getting rid of them!"

That certainly applied to Harry himself, the Duke thought somewhat cynically, and he wondered why, considering how dull it was, that he stayed on.

Now he was suspicious that it was not only because he hoped after all to be given a loan which would never be returned.

"I will take a look at the Library myself," the Duke decided.

Although he was an intelligent man, he admitted frankly that he would find it difficult to appraise the value of a book or to know if it was in fact as ancient as it appeared to be.

He was well aware that a great many fakes existed and he hoped that the Curator when he arrived would not raise his hopes over his discoveries only to find later that he had been mistaken.

"You have not much time!"

The Duke could almost hear a voice saying it in his ears.

He was aware that when the shooting-party came, including Colonel Ashurst and his daughter among his guests, he would find it very difficult to back out. The invitation itself was a moral commitment.

'Even so, if she is hideous or common, I definitely will not propose,' he thought as he walked towards the Library.

Then he saw Mr. Hansard advancing towards him down the long passage.

"I was just coming in search of Your Grace," Mr. Hansard said as the two men met. "I thought you would like to know that Mr. Baron whom we expected today has been unavoidably detained."

The Duke frowned.

"For how long?" he asked.

"I understand from his daughter it may be three or four days before he can reach here."

"His daughter?"

"Yes, Your Grace. I was just about to tell you that as Mr. Baron could not come himself at the last moment, he has sent his daughter to begin the work for him. She tells me she always works with her father and is very experienced."

"It is rather unususal work for a woman," the

Duke remarked, "but at least she can begin sorting out the books, which I imagine will take a long time."

"Oh, indeed, Your Grace. In fact Miss Baron was surprised at the size of the Library and the enormous number of volumes it contains."

"That is nothing new," the Duke remarked. "Give her every facility she needs for getting on with the task."

"I have already done everything possible that I can, Your Grace, but it is very unfortunate that her father was not able to arrive today, as we expected."

"I agree with you," the Duke replied. "I will go and see Miss Baron for myself, and tell her the quicker she gets down to work the better."

He spoke sharply and without waiting for Mr. Hansard to reply he walked on towards the Library.

He opened the door and for a moment as he looked down the long, perfectly proportioned room with a balcony along one side of it and the books making a pattern of colour from floor to ceiling, he thought it was empty.

Then he saw a slight movement at the third window on the left-hand side and moved forward.

The windows looked out over the green lawns which sloped down towards the lake.

There was crossing it at this particular point an exquisitely carved Chinese bridge which one of the Gorings had brought back with him from

Peking. Silhouetted against the water, it added an exotic touch to the English landscape that the Duke had always found strangely beautiful.

He saw now that there was a woman with her back to him looking at the view.

He could not see her face, but he was aware that she was very slight and had such a tiny waist that it could, in fashionable parlance, be "spanned by a man's two hands."

She wore nothing on her head, and her hair, which was a very pale gold that the Duke had seldom seen before, caught the last rays of the sinking sun.

It had been a grey day, but now there was a golden glow in the West which illuminated the horizon, and at the same time seemed to deepen the shadows of the oak trees in the Park.

The Duke had advanced to stand just behind the woman at the window before she either heard his footsteps on the thick Persian carpet, or she sensed his presence.

She turned around and he found himself looking into two large, pansy-coloured eyes that he thought to his astonishment had a touch of fear in them.

He was so surprised at her appearance, when he had expected somebody in her position to look quite different, that he could only stare at her without speaking, and she likewise stared at him until he saw the colour deepen very slowly in her cheeks.

It was then the Duke remembered his manners and remarked:

"You must be Miss Baron."

"Yes, Your Grace," Oletha replied and with an effort curtsied.

The Duke held out his hand.

"May I welcome you to Gore and say how sorry I am to learn from my secretary that your father is detained."

"He is . . . sorry too," Oletha answered, "but he told me to . . . start work on your Library. I must admit I had no idea it would be so . . . magnificent or contain so . . . many books."

The Duke smiled.

"I hope your father will not be dismayed at such a formidable task and that you will get to work immediately."

"Yes, of course, Your Grace," Oletha agreed, "but it seems extraordinary that it has not been catalogued before."

She spoke the words almost, the Duke thought, in the manner of a criticism and as if he felt he must excuse himself, he replied:

"I have only just come into possession of Gore, as I expect you realise, and one of the first things I have done is to ask for someone experienced to catalogue the Library."

"It must be very exciting for you!" Oletha exclaimed. "I wonder how many treasures of enormous value may be lying undiscovered on these shelves?"

She made a little gesture with her hand towards the books as she spoke which the Duke thought very graceful, and her long thin fingers might have been those of a ballet dancer.

"When do you intend to start?" he asked.

Then as if he could not prevent himself, he added:

"You are very young. Are you really knowledgeable in what I understand is very specialised work?"

"I hope I shall be able to satisfy Your Grace on that score by finding quickly some books that will delight you."

"What you are saying, Miss Baron," the Duke remarked, "is that 'the proof of the pudding is in the eating.' Very well, I am prepared to concede what is the obvious answer to my question. At the same time, I am in a hurry."

"Why is that?"

Oletha thought that her question coming so bluntly had surprised him.

He hesitated and she wondered if he would be frank with her and tell her the truth: that he wanted to sell anything that was valuable.

Then after a distinct pause the Duke said:

"Perhaps Mr. Hansard has already informed you that we have had a rather worrying letter from America."

He was quite certain that Mr. Hansard without his permission would have said nothing of the sort, but he told himself that he wanted to accelerate this girl's interest so that she would hurry to complete the work quicker than might normally be expected.

"Mr. Hansard did not mention anything about America," Oletha replied.

"We have had a letter telling us there is a rumour that the Library may contain a folio of Shakespeare."

"Surely if there was one you would be aware of it!" Oletha exclaimed.

"Incredibly the answer to that is 'no!'" the Duke said. "My father was not particularly interested in the books that have accumulated here over the centuries, while I, of course, have been abroad."

"If we find anything like that it would be very valuable," Oletha said quietly.

"I am aware of that," the Duke answered.

"And the Americans would pay a large sum for such a unique volume," she went on. "But I can hardly help feeling that as Shakespeare was English, his work should stay in this country."

"I did not say I was intending to sell it," the Duke said sharply.

Oletha looked at him and he thought that her strange eyes, which were different from any he had seen in a woman before, questioned whether he was telling the truth.

He looked away from her. Then an impulse he could not explain made him say:

"To be honest, Miss Baron, I hate to think of anything belonging to Gore being sold, but I need money and perhaps a Shakespeare folio would be the answer to some of my problems."

As he spoke he had the feeling she was glad he had not lied to her. It was not something he could explain, and yet it was there.

He looked at her and told himself she was so unexpectedly lovely that it would be difficult for any man not to talk about her rather than her work.

Then he asked:

"Surely you do not often stay away by yourself without your father? I should have thought it might be embarrassing for you to travel alone and visit strange houses without a chaperon."

"I only had to travel alone from London, Your Grace," Oletha replied, "and actually my father thought I would be perfectly safe for a few days at Gore before he could join me."

It struck the Duke that as she was so lovely it might be dangerous for her to be anywhere alone unless it was in a house where every man was blind.

Then he told himself he was being ridiculous and naturally somebody in Miss Baron's position was capable of looking after herself. She was not a Society girl who had to be cosseted and protected and never allowed out alone.

"We must get to work," he said sternly and had a feeling he was speaking to himself more than to her. "I am extremely anxious to see if you can find any reason why this strange rumour should have reached America. Incidentally my secretary has also had a similar letter from a well-known book-shop in London asking for first refusal of anything I wish to sell."

"You have not spoken of this to anyone?" Oletha asked.

"Nobody outside the house," the Duke replied.

Then he suddenly remembered that the other night at dinner his aunt had said:

"I hope I sleep better tonight than I did last night. The wind kept me awake."

"You should read," the elderly cousin with arthritis said. "It is something I always do when the pain in my legs keeps me awake."

"It is certainly an idea," his aunt answered. "I must find myself a good novel. I find Marie Corelli very soporific."

"There is plenty of choice in the Library," Harry interrupted, "and that reminds me, Sandor—some of those crumbling old volumes which have been there since the year dot would fetch a tidy sum on the market."

"What makes you think so?" the Duke enquired.

He thought Harry was going to reply, but he seemed to change his mind and instead started to talk about the latest novel by Miss Elinor Glyn which he said had shocked a great number of people who had read it.

So Harry had known the books were valuable, the Duke thought, and Harry had asked for the key of the Library!

Aloud he said:

"When you and your father have finished in here at the end of each day, Miss Baron, Mr. Hansard and I think it wise to keep the Library locked. So perhaps when you go upstairs you will take the key to his office? A footman will show you the way."

"Thank you, Your Grace, and I think you are wise. Books can be as valuable as pictures or jewels and people often forget that."

"Which do you prefer?" the Duke enquired.

She gave him a smile that seemed to illuminate her face.

"Being a woman I am allowed to be greedy and say that I would like to own all three!"

"It is not only women who are greedy."

"No, but they do not have to pretend to be high-souled as men are expected to be."

"Is that your impression?" the Duke asked. "I have always thought it is women who stand for high ideals, and are supposed to be a guide and an inspiration to mere men who follow where they lead."

He spoke with a cynical note in his voice which told Oletha that he did not believe a word he was saying.

She gave a little chuckle before she replied:

"I can see, Your Grace, that you have not been reading your own books. I have already noted on your shelves tales of dauntless courage and heroic sacrifice which have echoed down the history of mankind, and still happen today, if people will only look for them."

She was thinking as she spoke that her father had

told her that the Duke had been very brave and had fought on the North-West Frontier.

India and the difficulties of the British there had always fascinated Oletha, and she had read every book she could find on the subject. She had found the articles and descriptions of the fighting with the tribesmen that were often published in the *Illustrated London News* absorbing.

Almost as if the Duke could read her thoughts and there was no need for her to put them into words, he said:

"Are you thinking there are still deeds of valour taking place in parts of our Empire like India, Miss Baron?"

"How did you know I was thinking that?" she asked.

Then before the Duke could answer she added:

"Because you look almost as if you were still in uniform with the ragged barren rocks of the North-West Frontier just behind you."

She saw the surprise on his face and realised she had been speaking words which seemed to come into her mind without her really considering what she was saying.

"Are you interested in India?" the Duke enquired.

"It has always seemed to me to be a fascinating country, and I should love to go there," Oletha replied. "I have read everything I can find about it, including a History of Buddhism, and of course, the Vedas which have been translated."

"And you understand them?"

She gave him a shy little glance.

"You will think it presumptuous if I say yes, for as you are doubtless aware, they have defied many Scholars. But I try to read them with my heart rather than my mind, and I think sometimes I have been successful."

She spoke in a low voice almost as if she was talking to herself, and it was a moment before she realised that the Duke was staring at her incredulously.

"All the time I was in India," he said after a moment, "I never met a woman who bothered even to look at the translations of the ancient writings which to me have an indescribable beauty that I have never found anywhere else."

"I agree with you," Oletha said. "Something within me seems to respond to every word. Even if I do not get its exact meaning, yet emotionally I feel the beauty of it."

As she spoke she looked up at the Duke and there was no need for them to go on speaking to each other in words.

There was a long silence. Then abruptly, almost as if he called himself to attention, the Duke said:

"I feel, Miss Baron, that I am preventing you from getting down to work. Please concentrate on the more ancient volumes in the Library, and I shall be most interested to hear of your findings."

Without waiting for Oletha's reply he turned and walked away, moving swiftly as if he wished to put some distance between them.

Oletha watched him go and only as the Library

door closed behind him did she feel that she had been holding her breath.

So this was the Duke! This was the man who was prepared to marry her for her money!

She told herself that at first sight he had seemed awe-inspiring, cold, austere, and very frightening.

She thought that he was handsome in a rather strange manner, different from that of any other man she had ever seen.

Perhaps it was because his skin was sun-burnt from exposure to the hot sun, but also because his eyes were grey and strangely penetrating so that she felt when he looked at her, he saw through her pretence.

He was certainly very different from what she had expected. So different that it was impossible to explain it, even to herself.

It was almost as if some power within him had compelled her to speak as she had, to tell him the truth of her feelings as she thought now she would never have spoken of them to anybody else.

She had the uncomfortable feeling that her heart was beating rather fast and it was difficult to breathe naturally.

But why?

She asked the question and was afraid of the answer.

Chapter Four

OLETHA FOUND it difficult to sleep even though her bedroom was very comfortable, if somewhat shabby.

She realised that as the Curator's daughter she was sleeping on the Second Floor in what she told herself were second-class bedrooms.

Nevertheless they were large and attractive and there was opening out of her bedroom a Sitting-Room where, as she had expected, she would eat alone.

Because she was determined to find out everything she could about the Duke, she talked first to the House-keeper who had shown her where she was to sleep.

"Have you been here a long time, Mrs. Fellows?" she enquired.

"I have indeed, Miss. Forty years next month, and I've seen many changes during my time, and few for the better."

Oletha listened knowing this was a prelude to hearing Mrs. Fellows' personal history and she was not disappointed.

She heard how Mrs. Fellows had come when she was a young girl to work in the house as her mother had done before her.

"Things were very grand then when the third Duke was alive," she related. "There were twelve footmen always on duty in white wigs and wearing white gloves that had to be laundered every day, and it was nothing for us to have a party of forty or fifty people staying in the house."

"It must have been very exciting!" Oletha exclaimed.

"It was a lot of hard work, Miss, and that's the truth, but there were as many valets and lady's maids staying so there was, so to speak, a party downstairs as well as up."

"Does the present Duke entertain so lavishly?" Oletha asked, knowing the answer.

"No, indeed not, Miss," Mrs. Fellows replied. "Things aren't what they used to be, and from all I hears His Grace has inherited a pile of debts as well as a lot of repairs that should have been done years ago."

"Do you mean that the estate has been neglected?" Oletha asked, with a surprised air. "It looks very impressive."

"That's 'cos you've just arrived, Miss, and not seen things as we sees them," Mrs. Fellows said firmly. "There's tiles off the roof, cracks in the walls, besides curtains that are in tatters, and carpets so threadbare you can catch your toe in them."

Oletha was amused by the consternation in the House-keeper's tone, but because she wished to sound ignorant on such matters she remarked:

"I am surprised. I thought all Dukes were very rich."

"They were in the past, Miss, but things have changed and there's a lot of noblemen feeling the pinch these days, which is why as I understands from the newspapers they often marry Americans from across the Atlantic."

"Yes," Oletha agreed. "I heard that the Duke of Marlborough had married an American wife, and the Duke of Leinster."

"Let's hope they're happy, Miss, but I doubts it."

"Why?" Oletha asked.

"Because Americans don't think the same as we do," Mrs. Fellows said with a touch of scorn in her voice, "and I can't see His Grace having anything in common with such ladies, rich though they may be."

"What sort of lady do you think His Grace is likely to admire?" Oletha asked.

Mrs. Fellows laughed.

"Unless he's changed in the years he's been

away, Miss, he'll have plenty of choice. There were always ladies after him when he was a mere boy, but then he were always a handsome one."

"Then why has he never married?"

"I expect he felt he couldn't afford to, Miss, not on a soldier's pay. His late Grace was never over-generous, not even to Master George, the young Marquis."

"So the present Duke before he inherited had to scrimp and save," Oletha remarked.

"That's a fact, Miss. I've even heard him say to Mr. Bateson—that's the Butler—'Lend me a couple of pounds, Bateson. I haven't a penny in my pocket and I have to go to London this afternoon.'"

It seemed to Oletha rather extraordinary, but it was very much as her father had told her.

"Are you pleased that the present Duke is the one who inherited?" she asked.

It was a question to which she wanted an answer and which Mrs. Fellows was delighted to give to her.

"To tell the truth, Miss, I always hoped Master Sandor would be the one. His brother, poor lad, was always ailing. Sickly he was from the time he was born. But Master Sandor was a regular Hercules and everyone on the estate thought the world of him. It's real glad we are to have him home."

There was no doubt, Oletha thought when she was alone, that Mrs. Fellows at any rate, gave the Duke a good reference.

But there was still a great deal more she wanted to know about a man before she married him, especially one who was only interested in what she had in the Bank.

She thought first of how angry her father would be if he knew where she was at this moment, and secondly she tried to make up her mind about the Duke and what she had felt when she saw him.

He was very different from what she had expected, and yet at the same time, she found it difficult to explain the difference even to herself.

'Perhaps I am imagining it,' she thought, when morning came and she got out of bed and started to dress.

It was not yet seven o'clock when she came from her room and went down the stairs.

The house-maids in their mob-caps who were busy brushing and dusting looked at her in surprise, as did the footmen working in their shirtsleeves, but wearing striped waist-coats with silver-crested buttons that were part of their uniform.

Oletha bade them good-morning and went out of the front door into the crisp air that had a touch of frost in it.

She was wrapped warmly in a coat that was lined with fur and had a small sable collar which encircled her throat.

She thought perhaps it was a rather expensive and rich-looking garment to be worn by a Curator's daughter, but it would have been impossible under Martha's eagle eye to take with her anything that was old or too plain when she was supposed to be staying with Lady Grayson.

"The Duke, if I meet him, will not notice my clothes," she told herself.

She had already ascertained the whereabouts of the stables and she walked briskly towards them, entering by an arched gateway to find, as she had expected, a long line of stalls on either side of a cobbled yard.

If the house was dilapidated the stables were not and had obviously been recently painted.

The tops of the doors had been opened and there were a number of horses looking out.

Oletha immediately recognised their quality and went from one horse to another, patting and inspecting them, and wishing her father was with her. She was sure he would be able to remember the breeding of all those who were outstanding.

"Good-morning, Ma'am!"

One of the grooms had joined her without her being aware of it and she smiled at him as he added:

"Oi see ye're admiring Red Duster. 'A magnificent horse!' That's what His Grace always says, an' if ye'll excuse me, Ma'am, Oi must be saddling him, as His Grace'll be wishin' to ride him."

Oletha stood to one side, and as the groom entered the stall, she thought it would be a mistake to encounter the Duke so early in the morning and she had better walk elsewhere.

But she could not resist just stepping into the stall to take another look at Red Duster, and then it was too late!

"Good-morning, Miss Baron!" a voice said behind her. 'Are you as knowledgeable about horses as you are about books?"

It was the Duke who spoke and as Oletha turned to look at him she thought that in his riding-breeches and highly polished boots he looked even more handsome and awe-inspiring than he had yesterday.

"I love horses!" she said simply, "and those I have seen in your stables are certainly outstanding!"

"I have a feeling," the Duke said, "that you would like to ride one of them."

Oletha's eyes lit up, then remembering who she was supposed to be, she said:

"Perhaps you would think I was . . . neglecting the work which is . . . waiting for me in the . . . Library."

"It is still very early in the morning," the Duke said, "and I realise the English do not start at cock-crow as we were obliged to do in India."

"Then may I ride with you?" Oletha asked.

"I will wait for ten minutes!" the Duke said. "If you are longer I fear you will have to find your way alone."

Oletha did not reply but merely gave him a smile and lifting her skirt ran across the cobbled yard towards the house.

Knowing her father did not like being kept waiting, she was used to changing her clothes in a hurry, although as she ran up the stairs she thought she would miss Martha.

Fortunately one of the house-maids was in her room when she entered it, having brought her an early morning cup of tea, and was surprised to find she had already gone.

"Please help me," Oletha begged, and began to take off her coat and the gown beneath it.

Martha had not only packed a habit, she had packed two of them. Oletha chose the one which was tight-bodiced and modelled in the fashion the Empress of Austria had made the vogue when she was hunting in the Shires.

It gave her an exquisite figure and not only made her waist seem extraordinarily small, but outlined the soft, almost immature curves of her breasts.

Quickly Oletha put many more hair-pins into her hair which she had already arranged neatly at the back of her head and placed on it a smart top-hat.

She still had two minutes to spare as she ran down the stairs and out through the front door.

As she had expected, there was a groom waiting at the foot of the steps with the horse she was to ride and the Duke was walking his own mount round the gravel sweep.

Oletha put her foot into the stirrup and seemed almost to fly into the saddle. The groom arranged her skirt, and then she lifted her reins and rode up to the Duke.

"Nine minutes and I think about fifty-one seconds!" she said.

"I must certainly commend you for your punctuality!"

"You sound as if you were going to add: 'if for nothing else!'" Oletha said accusingly. "It makes me more determined than ever to confound you with the treasures I shall unearth in the Library."

"I am certainly hoping you will do that," the Duke answered, "but I told myself last night it is a mistake to hope that the gods will be so generous when they have given me so much already."

He looked at the Park in front of him as he spoke, and Oletha knew he was thinking how fortunate he was to have become the Duke of Gorleston.

"I am sure that from the time you were a small boy you wished it could be yours as it is now," she said softly.

He looked at her in surprise.

"Why should you think that?"

"Because there is nobody, especially someone whose name is Goring, who would not want to own Gore. It is without exception, the most magnificent house I have ever imagined."

"That is what I want it to continue to be."

"So if I am successful in my treasure-hunt,

Gore will be saved."

"Shall we say that many things which need to be done could be paid for?"

The Duke thought as he spoke that this was a most extraordinary conversation to be having with a strange young girl, and he changed the subject in the same abrupt manner he had done yesterday.

"I think we should gallop and get some of the exuberance out of our mounts," he said.

It was true the horses had been fidgeting a little and pulling at their bits, but not unduly so. Oletha was well aware that this was an excuse not to go on talking to her.

At the same time she had discovered something she wanted to know: that Gore meant a great deal to the Duke, perhaps even more than his freedom.

Then as she galloped beside him, the horses' hoofs throwing out pieces of turf behind them, she told herself that she was nevertheless somewhat skeptical.

There was a great deal of talk about his not being able to live in the same style as his father had done, but was it really as bad as he made out?

Perhaps she would discover when she delved further that his interest lay in amusements of a different kind from those which had been his father's.

He might enjoy horses, but perhaps he did not

care for racing. He might want money so that he could spend more time in London.

That would not seem unreasonable after he had been abroad for seven years.

She could not quite visualise him as a 'Stage-Door Johnny' taking out one of the glamorous and notorious Gaiety Girls for supper at Romano's—still one never knew!

Because she was an only child Oletha had spent an unusual amount of time alone with her father or accompanied by his friends of his own age.

Although she was not allowed to go to balls or dine downstairs when there was a large dinner-party, often, if her father had only two or three contemporaries to stay, she dined with them.

The Colonel usually sent her to bed when the gentlemen came from the Dining-Room, but because they looked upon her as a child, they said things in front of her which they would not have said had they thought of her as grown up.

"Have you heard Reggie's got himself tangled up with a chorus-girl who's taking every penny he possesses off him?" one of her father's friends had asked.

"I have seen her. She is worth everything Reggie can give her," another of her father's cronies laughed.

"Nevertheless he is a fool!" the Colonel said positively. "If his wife had any sense she would put her foot down!"

"Not a chance of that," was the reply, "even if Enid does hold the purse-strings."

"She must grow tired of seeing her money being spent on the sort of women Reggie admires," the Colonel said sharply.

"I think if the truth were known she is fed up with Reggie, but he will stick to her because he cannot afford to do otherwise, and she enjoys being a Countess."

That conversation came back to Oletha now and she told herself if that was the future, she would have to endure if she married the Duke, she would never, whatever her father might say, consent to be his wife.

She glanced at him from under her eye-lashes as the horses settled down to a trot, and she thought he did not look the type of man who would run after chorus-girls. Yet how did she know what men liked?

How could one judge a man on how he appeared against the background of Gore and amid an admiring crowd of old retainers to tell him and anyone else who would listen how wonderful he was?

'It will soon make him extremely conceited,' Oletha thought.

Because she suddenly wanted, in a way she could not understand, to hurt him, she said:

"I cannot help wondering, Your Grace, why you are trying to sell the treasures that your ancestors have accumulated over the centuries. Could you not work to find the money you need?"

She meant to startle the Duke and she succeeded.

He turned to look at her and she saw the surprise in his grey eyes, before he asked:

"Work? What do you mean by work?"

"I am well aware that for gentlemen work is beneath their condescension," Oletha replied, "but I have always been told that Americans, because they worked hard, made great fortunes, and I believe many Englishmen have come back from India far richer than when they arrived in that country."

"That was true of those who served in the East Indian Company at the beginning of the century," the Duke agreed, "but it is not easy now to become wealthy unless one is corrupt."

The way he said the word told Oletha that was something he would not contemplate in any circumstances.

As if she had started a train of thought within his mind he went on:

"For Americans it is different. The pioneers found an underdeveloped country with unlimited natural resources. Those who were intelligent like the Astors, bought land later made exceedingly valuable, while others found treasure which automatically made them millionaires."

"You are speaking of those who found oil on their property," Oletha said, thinking of her grandfather.

"Exactly!" the Duke said. "But I have in the past, had no money to invest either in land or stocks and shares and so my only assets are not negotiable."

"You have, of course, your health and strength," Oletha said, "and perhaps a brain that is even more valuable."

Again the Duke looked at her and there was a distinct twinkle in his eyes, as he said:

"I have a feeling, Miss Baron, that you are gunning for me, and I cannot think why, unless you disapprove of me for some reason I cannot ascertain."

"I would not dare to do anything so presumptuous," Oletha replied quickly.

Almost despite herself there was a note of mockery in her voice.

The Duke noticed it and he said:

"So you do disapprove of me. That is interesting and I would like to understand why."

"Your Grace is twisting what I said quite casually into something far more serious than I intended," Oletha said evasively.

Because she felt she had been indiscreet and wished to avoid pursuing the subject, she touched her horse with her heel and as he bounded forward, the Duke had to quicken the pace of his own mount to keep up with her.

It was sometime later when they had turned for home that he said:

"I have been thinking over what you said, Miss

Baron, and I suppose because your father works hard in his chosen profession, you expect other men to follow his example. But quite frankly, the only occupation I have been trained for is the Army, and I have always been told that old soldiers are a glut on the market, so there is nothing for them to do but fade into obscurity."

"That is something you would never be able to do, Your Grace."

Oletha looked not at him as she spoke, but at Gore and the magnificent picture the house presented ahead of them, touched by a very pale sun breaking through the clouds.

It illuminated the many windows, turning them to gold, and it seemed too to light up the high chimneys and the vast expanse of roof silhouetted against the sky.

It was so lovely and at the same time so majestic that Oletha said as if the words came from her heart:

"You cannot . . . lose that."

"That is what I was thinking," the Duke agreed, "and as you have already said, I must work in every way that I can to keep it."

The way he spoke made Oletha feel almost as if he took a vow.

Then she knew that without really intending it she had driven him into making a decision to marry in order to preserve Gore.

She wanted to cry out that that was not what she had meant, and when she had suggested he might work, she had thought of him working with his hands and with his brain, achieving something on his own which did not depend on his noble birth.

Instead her instinct told her that he was now thinking of marriage as a means by which he could work for Gore and the estate, and he had now committed himself to a course of action on which, until her arrival, he had still been undecided.

"Fool! Fool!" she wanted to cry at herself.

Then she knew that the casting vote was still in her own hands.

If, when her counterfeit visit came to an end and she decided not to marry the Duke, she would find a way, however impossible it now seemed, to avoid having to join the party to which he had invited her father and "his rich daughter!"

They rode on in silence and Oletha was aware that the Duke was deep in his thoughts.

Only as they reached the front of the house did he say conventionally:

"I hope your ride has been as enjoyable as you expected, Miss Baron."

"It has indeed, Your Grace! I am very grateful," Oletha replied.

"I hope you will feel free to ask for a horse whenever you want one," he said courteously.

Two stable-lads came running towards them and as the Duke dismounted Oletha wondered whether he would help her from the saddle, but he allowed her to reach the ground unattended and was already half-way up the steps to the front door before she joined him.

"If you have anything to show me, Miss Baron," he said in what she thought was now a different tone of voice, "Mr. Hansard will always know where to find me."

"Thank you, Your Grace," Oletha said quietly.

She started to climb the staircase, wishing as she did so, that the Duke, who she was sure was going to the Breakfast-Room, would invite her to come with him.

But he handed his hat, gloves and whip to one of the footmen and walked across the Hall without looking back at her.

As she went up the stairs she did not understand why, but she felt curiously depressed, almost as if she had been reading a book and found disappointingly that it had an unhappy ending.

Oletha was in the Library inspecting the books, looking to see if by some chance there was, if not the Shakespeare folio, at least something rare and valuable.

Because she hoped to find something quickly to please the Duke, she was making no effort to start cataloguing as she knew Mr. Baron would have done on arrival.

Instead she was just examining the shelves,

finding there was very little order or arrangement on any of them.

She would sometimes find a book that had only been published two or three years earlier, next to one that had been printed in the 16th century, or a manuscript that was faded and tattered, although on examination, it proved not to be as old as its appearance suggested.

She had begun to think the talk about there being an undiscovered gold-mine on the shelves in the Library was nothing but a rumour.

She heard the Library door open and felt excitedly that it was the Duke. It would be a relief to talk to him and perhaps duel in words as they had this morning, even though she regretted the way in which it had ended.

Then she saw that coming towards her down the long room, was a man she had never seen before.

He was tall and dark, and she thought, although she was not sure, that he bore a vague resemblance to the Duke. However, the stranger was by no means so good-looking and had a somewhat dilettante appearance which was certainly something no-one could say about the Duke.

As he reached her she saw the surprise in his eyes and realised it was because of her appearance.

"I heard there was a Curator coming to Gore!"

he exclaimed, "but I did not expect it to be a woman, or indeed anyone so lovely!"

His surprise and the way he spoke seemed to Oletha amusing and she said demurely:

"Good-morning, Sir. Actually the Curator is my father, but as he was detained I came ahead of him."

The man standing before her with his eyes still on her face held out his hand.

"Let me introduce myself," he said, "I am Captain Harry Goring, the Duke's cousin, and now I know you are Miss Baron, so let me say how delighted I am to meet you."

Oletha put her hand in his, then as he held it a little longer than was necessary, she decided she did not like the Duke's cousin.

There was something about him that she could not pin-point, and yet was quite certain it was unpleasant.

Her father had often chided her for the way she made up her mind, as he thought, too quickly about anyone she met.

"How can you possibly say that you dislike General Burns' nephew?" he had asked only a few weeks ago as they were riding home from a visit to a near neighbour. "You talked to him for only about ten minutes."

"It was long enough for me to know that I have no wish to further my acquaintance with him and that if I were the General I would lock up the silver spoons before he leaves!"

Oletha spoke jokingly, but her father answered angrily:

"These hasty judgements are quite ridiculous and not at all becoming in a young girl!"

"You have often asked me in the past what I thought about people, Papa, and you have always admitted that although you have challenged what I said at the time, I have invariably been proved right."

The Colonel was silent because he knew it was true. He thought to himself that Oletha had an uncanny way of looking into the depths of a man or woman's character, almost as soon as she met them.

At the same time, he thought it was an undesirable accomplishment in someone so young, and aloud he said:

"I think it is a habit you should not cultivate, and instead you should accept people at their face value."

"I assure you that is what I want to do," Oletha replied, "but just sometimes I find myself knowing that beneath the face they show to the world there is a very different personality, and one which is invariably unpleasant."

Because she wanted to do what her father wished and be exactly the type of daughter that he wanted, she had deliberately gone out of her way not to use what she called her "perceptive sense."

Now, without even thinking about it, that sense told her that the Duke's cousin, Harry Goring, was not what he appeared to be.

"How could I imagine," he was saying, "that Curators looked like you? I assure you after this, I shall haunt every Library and in fact, every Museum, wondering what I shall find."

"You are very flattering," Oletha answered, "but I am afraid, Captain Goring, I cannot stop and talk as there is a great deal of work to be done and I want to get started before my father arrives."

"It will take both of you years to catalogue all the books there are here," Harry replied, "and that means there will be plenty of time for us to talk together and to get to know each other. Let me add, Miss Baron, that is something I very much want to do."

Oletha thought he was determined to flirt with her, but she was also determined that she would not encourage him.

She took a book from one of the shelves, seeing that it was a finely bound volume of poems by Lord Byron, but was not particularly rare.

"Have you found Shakespeare's folio yet?" Harry Goring enquired.

"No," Oletha replied uncompromisingly.

"It will be very thrilling when you do so."

"I very much doubt the folio will be here."

"Why do you say that?"

"Because if it were here, there would surely

have been some knowledge of its existence in the last hundred years or so."

"I imagine my cousin has told you there is a strong rumour that it is at Gore, and in fact there are collectors in America who would be willing to buy it."

It struck Oletha as surprising that he should know so much about it, and also there was undoubtedly a greedy note in his voice.

She was aware that Captain Goring had come a little closer to her.

"I have something to suggest to you, Miss Baron," he said. "I feel you are a sport and will help me to surprise my cousin as I wish to do."

Oletha did not answer but he knew that while she turned the pages of the book she was holding in her hand, she was listening.

"It is the Duke's birthday in a week or so," Harry went on, "and I can think of nothing that would please him more than if the folio was found. I am certain it is here somewhere, and we could present it to him as a surprise."

Even as he spoke Oletha saw almost as if she was looking into a crystal ball, exactly what Captain Goring was scheming to do.

Because she could hardly believe her own conviction that he was crooked she asked:

"What are you suggesting?"

She raised her eyes as she spoke with what she hoped was an innocent expression of trust in them.

"You *are* a sport!" he exclaimed. "Now this is what we will do, Miss Baron. The moment you find the folio, you tell no-one but me. Then I will have it packed up in a very special parcel and when the Duke's birthday arrives we will hand it to him first thing in the morning, after he has had his breakfast."

Oletha said nothing and Harry Goring went on:

"Can you imagine how thrilled he will be? I do not know what the market price for a Shakespearean folio is, but I am sure in New York there will be a dozen bidders to out-vie each other in their anxiety to possess anything so rare."

"Perhaps it would be . . . wrong," Oletha said a little hesitatingly, "should I make such an . . . exciting discovery, not to tell the Duke . . . who is employing my . . . father and me . . . immediately. . . ."

"And spoil the surprise?" Harry Goring asked. "Now I can see you are a very intelligent as well as a very lovely young woman. You know as well as I do that no present could give my cousin more pleasure than one which will enable him to carry out many of the repairs which are vitally needed here in the family house."

"Yes . . . I can see . . . that," Oletha agreed a little doubtfully.

"You and I are going to be partners in this," Harry insisted, "and I promise you, if you do as I ask and allow me to make my cousin a very happy man, then I will give you something that you will want to treasure always."

He moved still nearer to her as he spoke.

"I think turquoises, which are always considered lucky, would look lovely against your white skin."

Oletha turned to put the book of Byron's poems back onto the shelf and managed as she did so, to take a step away from him.

"Is that agreed?" he asked, and she knew he was uncertain of her reply.

"I would like to think about it, Captain Goring. Although I understand you want to please your cousin, I feel my father would not approve of my doing anything that was not completely aboveboard."

"Oh, come on now!" Harry Goring coaxed. "I cannot believe you will let me down and spoil my surprise."

"There is always the possibility to be considered," Oletha said, "that I will find nothing and that the whole idea was just a rumour."

She saw the disappointment on Harry's face and knew he had a very personal interest in finding the folio.

"Well, you turn over these old volumes as quickly as you can," he said, "and I am quite certain you will come up with something. You are too pretty not to be lucky."

"I shall certainly do my best."

"If your best comes up trumps, which I am

116

sure it will, you will not let your partner down?"

"I have already said I will think about it."

"Then think about the turquoises I am going to give you. Anyone as lovely as you should have jewels, and I want to be the first to make you glitter with them."

"You are . . . very kind," Oletha murmured.

"That is what I want to be," Harry said.

He looked over his shoulder, then he said, lowering his voice:

"What about meeting me in the garden this evening before dinner? There is a little arbour at the end of the long lawn behind some bushes. If you go before it is dark you will find your way quite easily and I will bring you home safely."

Oletha did not look at him in case he should see the expression in her eyes. Instead she said:

"That is something else I should like to think about, Captain Goring."

"I shall be waiting for you," he said, "and I promise you will not be disappointed."

He glanced over his shoulder again and she had the feeling he was afraid someone might come into the Library and find him there.

As he looked back at her again she had a distinct feeling of danger.

She was aware as he said the words aloud, that he was thinking whether he should try to kiss her now, or whether he should wait until this evening.

Oletha took another step away from where

they had been standing and as if he made up his mind, Harry Goring said:

"Do not forget, I will be waiting in the arbour at five-thirty. You should have finished by then."

He did not wait for her answer, but walked in a jaunty manner down the Library and out through the door, shutting it behind him.

Only when he had gone did Oletha draw in a deep breath and realised she had escaped by a hair's breadth from having to struggle in an undignified manner with a man whom she both disliked and despised.

She had the feeling that he could be dangerous not only to her but to the Duke.

She was quite certain that if she handed over the folio to him to give to his cousin as a birthday surprise, both the folio and Harry Goring would vanish, and she wondered if she ought to warn the Duke of the suggestion he had made to her.

Then she knew it was unlikely that he would believe her. If challenged, Captain Goring would undoubtedly say that he had only been thinking of how he could please the Duke, and of course he had every intention of making it a genuine birthday surprise.

'I shall say nothing, but I must certainly be on my guard,' Oletha decided.

She had luncheon alone which she found somewhat depressing, and she kept thinking how much more exciting it would have been to be with the Duke, even if Harry Goring was with him.

The moment she finished she went back to the Library to start again turning over book after book. She found one or two which would be, she knew, extremely interesting to scholars, but certainly had not the value of a folio of Shakespeare.

She began after several hours' work to think despairingly that there was no doubt that she had been right in what she had said to Harry Goring. The whole idea was just a rumour which might have been started by him in the first place.

Then as she put back one book almost angrily because it was not in the least what she was hoping to find, she once again heard the Library door open and this time when she looked round she saw that her visitor was the Duke.

She knew as she saw him come towards her that she had been hoping for hours which had somehow seemed like centuries, that he would come to see how she was getting on.

Now, as he drew nearer she felt her heart beating in a strange fashion and it struck her as quite extraordinary how glad she was that he was there.

Her eyes met his grey ones as he stopped a few feet away from her, and she had the strange feeling that he had come to her because he had been unable to keep away.

Chapter Five

OLETHA WENT into her bedroom and shut the door.

It had been an amusing evening, more amusing than any evening she had ever spent before.

When the Duke had asked her if she would dine with him and Captain Goring, she had felt an irrepressible joy that he wanted her.

At the same time, she had known that had he considered her a lady and his equal, she would not have been invited to dine with him unchaperoned.

She told herself that having started on this career of deceit she could not complain if the Duke believed her to be the daughter of a Curator and so unimportant socially that she could stay away alone in a strange house without even en-quiring if there was an older woman who would make her presence respectable.

Resolutely she refused to think of anything but the excitement of dining with the Duke, knowing because it was something she had never done before in her life, it would taste, like all forbidden fruit, extremely sweet.

She had taken a great deal of trouble in choos-ing what gown she would wear.

All her gowns were comparatively simple be-cause she was not yet a débutante, but they were all extremely expensive, and their simplicity lay not in their design and making, but in their being less ostentatiously ornamented than was the fash-ion at the moment.

Nevertheless, the full skirt, the tiny waist and the close-fitting bodice swathed around the shoul-ders with tulle was exceedingly becoming.

Oletha's white skin showed to its best advan-tage when her shoulders were bare, and her long neck gave her a grace that made every other woman seem clumsy in comparison.

She finally chose a gown that was her father's favourite. It was white and the ribbons which ornamented the skirt were pale love-in-a-mist blue. She tied a bow of the same ribbon at the top of her heavy chignon of plaited hair which was pinned to the top of her head.

She looked young, innocent, and untouched, yet at the same time she had an undeniable *chic* which the average girl of her age would have been unable to achieve.

As she walked down the staircase, knowing that she was in fact doing something outrageous from a social point of view, she felt as if she was taking part in a play and that the curtain was rising on the Second Act.

How the whole drama would end she did not dare speculate even to herself. She only knew an excitement that made her feel as if there were wings on her feet and her eyes were full of stars.

"Later," she told herself, "if I have to be punished for my misdeeds, I will not complain!"

The Duke was alone in the Blue Salon where the Butler had told her they were to meet before dinner.

She could not help wondering if he had chosen that particular room because the blue brocade on the walls and the blue of the curtains was the perfect background for the gold of her hair.

Then she told herself she was assuming an importance she could not presume to have.

The Duke was only being kind because he wanted her to find the books which could mean so much to him and perhaps affect his whole future, and there was nothing deeper or more personal in his invitation.

That was what her brain told her, but her heart beating in a strange way was telling her something very different.

She walked towards him over the exquisitely

patterned carpet, and the lighted candles in the crystal chandeliers shone on her hair.

She had learned from the maid who dressed her that at night the Duke preferred to use candlelight rather than the new electric lighting which his father had installed at great expense.

"Candlelight!" Oletha had exclaimed. "That is more becoming to a woman than any other sort of illumination."

"It will certainly be becoming to you, Miss, with your gold hair," the maid said. "In fact, I think in that beautiful gown you look like a fairy Princess!"

Oletha had smiled at the compliment.

Now as she walked down the Blue Salon she wondered if the Duke thought she was anything but a useful employee he wished to stimulate into more successful efforts than had been achieved so far.

He watched her all the way down the room and she was acutely conscious of his eyes on her.

Then as she came to a stop a few feet away from him and looked up into his face, she was suddenly still.

She felt as if everything, even the room and all its contents, had vanished and they were alone; two people meeting across time and space in a mystic manner that she could not put into words.

It seemed as if the Duke had nothing to say either, but only stood looking at her, his eyes penetrating and very grey in his sunburned face.

Oletha felt as if he looked deep into her soul.

Then, when for a moment of time they had touched eternity, the door opened and Harry Goring came in to join them.

"Surely I am not late!" he exclaimed. "I have no intention of missing a glass of champagne, Sandor!"

"Of course not!" the Duke replied automatically, but his voice sounded as if it came from a great distance.

As he spoke the Butler appeared in the doorway with a bottle of champagne in a cooler and behind him came a footman with crystal glasses on a silver tray.

After that it seemed to Oletha as if the play in which she had imagined she was performing was enacted by three people who executed their parts faultlessly.

In the small Dining-Room, where the walls were the pale green that Adam had made peculiarly his own, the lighting came from two magnificent candelabra on the table and four others, equally magnificent, on side-tables.

The candle-light flickered on the faces of the Goring ancestors which decorated the walls, and softened the hardness of their features so that they did not look critical or accusing, but positively benign.

The Duke sat at the head of the table, in a

huge high-backed arm-chair, which was ornamented with his coat-of-arms.

To Oletha he seemed to become one with the portraits of his forebears so that the past and present were united in him, and the only question was: what of the future?

Because Harry Goring was with them it was difficult to be introspective or even serious.

He was too clever at being what was almost a professional entertainer not to play the role that was expected of him and make them laugh.

He told stories about the Goring family and their idiosyncracies, and even more amusing tales about the people he knew in London.

Because the Duke had been abroad for so long they were as new to him as they were to Oletha, and because Harry was a good raconteur he made them seem real, human, and very amusing so that they laughed and went on laughing as he wished them to do.

Only when the excellent dinner was finished and the servants had withdrawn from the Dining-Room did Harry lift his glass and say:

"I think, Sandor, we should drink a toast to our charming guest, and wish her luck in her search for hidden treasure which so far continues regrettably to remain a myth rather than a reality."

"Of course," the Duke replied, "I was just going to suggest it myself."

He lifted his own glass as he spoke and as he did so, he said:

"In the circumstances a toast to 'Miss Baron' seems rather formal, but you have not yet told me your name."

The Duke was looking at Oletha as he spoke. She was very conscious of his eyes and what she hoped was an expression of admiration in them, so she replied without thinking:

"My name is Oletha."

Even as she spoke she had a terrifying feeling that she had been indiscreet, and that the name, because it was so unusual, would make the Duke question her identity.

Then as she saw his expression did not change, she knew with relief that he was not aware that was the name of the girl he had invited to stay next weekend with his father's old friend.

"An unusual name," he remarked lightly, "but a very charming one!"

"As beautiful as its owner," Harry Goring added looking at her flirtatiously.

But Oletha was still watching the Duke, thinking that it might have been a disastrous slip on her part to have given her real name.

Because she was enjoying herself so much, she had, for the moment, completely forgotten that she was not herself but a fictitious character who might have stepped out of one of the books she had been examining all afternoon.

"To Oletha!" the Duke was saying, "and may she bring this house good fortune and of course, happiness."

"To Oletha!" Harry cried, making the name sound dramatic.

Then he drank, but while his eyes were seeking hers she deliberately looked away from him.

"Thank . . . you," she said a little shyly. "I can only hope that I shall not . . . disappoint you."

After dinner when they sat in the Salon and continued talking but mostly listening to Harry, Oletha had a sudden longing to be alone with the Duke.

There were so many things, she thought, that she wished to talk to him about, and although it was impossible not to laugh at what Harry was saying, she would have much preferred to ask the Duke questions about India, and if he had read the books she had found so fascinating.

But there was no opportunity of that for Harry never left them. Yet she had the unmistakable feeling that the Duke felt the same way as she did.

"I expect I am imagining it," she told herself a little despondently, "and in fact, if he had wanted to talk to me alone, he could have done so when he came to the Library."

He had actually merely asked her if she would dine downstairs, then after a few perfunctory questions as to what she had discovered he had left her, even though she had longed for him to stay.

She looked at him now sitting on the other side of the hearth-rug and thought how fascinating it would be if he would not only tell her about his past, but talk with her about the future.

When they had ridden together there had seemed to be an intimacy between them which she thought he was now deliberately avoiding, and it was almost as if he was afraid of her.

The evening had been an exciting one, but when she reluctantly suggested that she should retire to bed, the Duke had made no effort to persuade her to stay.

'I like him,' Oletha thought in the quietness of her bedroom. 'I like him . . . very much.'

Then there was a question in her mind to which she did not wish to reply.

The maid came when she rang the bell and helped her to undress. When she took the pins from her hair and undid the plait, it fell over her shoulders like a cascade of heavy gold.

"Your hair's quite a different colour from any I've ever seen before, Miss," the maid said.

"I have always been told I inherited it from a Swedish ancestor," Oletha replied.

"That would explain it!" the maid exclaimed. "You don't look English and that's a fact, Miss!"

Oletha smiled to herself.

She had often imagined when she had seen herself in the mirror with her hair hanging over her shoulders and reaching to her waist that she in some way resembled the Sirens who had tried to entice Ulysses into danger, and to evade them he had himself roped to the mast of his ship.

'I wonder if the Duke regards me as a Siren?' she thought.

Then she told herself she was being very conceited.

"He hopes I will be useful to him, and that is the reason why he is being so pleasant, not because, like Captain Goring, he wishes to flirt with me."

The Captain had certainly been very effusive all the evening, and yet Oletha had been aware that his charm was only surface deep.

"He is greedy and grasping," she told herself now, "and if he could cheat the Duke out of the Shakespeare folio or anything else, he would do so. Well, he shall not have it!"

She laughed because she was making this search for treasure a personal matter, and yet, she asked herself, was it anything else?

Supposing she found the treasure for the Duke? What would it mean to her?

Would he in the circumstances cancel the invitation he had extended to her father to shoot at Gore next Saturday?

'There is only tomorrow to find what he is seeking,' she thought in a sudden panic.

When the maid had gone she got into bed, but she found it impossible to sleep.

Instead she kept wondering what the Duke would feel if she found what he wanted, and if she did not find it what he would say when she arrived with her father and he realised who she was.

The real question was whether, having seen him, she would accept the invitation to be his guest as the rich heiress who would save Gore, or whether she would somehow contrive that whatever her father might say, she would never see him again.

She did not know the answer; she only played in her mind with the different possibilities between which she alone had the choice.

Then as she lay in the darkness a sudden idea came to her, almost as if it was a message from some force outside herself.

She had been talking to the Duke during dinner while for a few minutes Harry was concentrating on his food and not trying to make them laugh.

"This room is so beautiful," she had said, "and the walls blend so perfectly with the more brilliant colours in the portraits of your ancestors."

"That is something I have always thought," the Duke replied, "and in every room in this house where we have kept to the original colours chosen by Adam himself, the results are, to my mind at any rate, perfect."

"I think colour is very important," Oletha agreed, "and when I am in the Library I always think that nothing could be more decorative than the bindings of the books in that particular setting."

The Duke smiled agreement. Then he said:

"I remember how furious my father was many years ago when he had an old friend to stay who had been a Professor at Oxford University and in his old age had taken up book-binding."

"As a hobby?" Oletha enquired.

"I can assure you no-one would have employed him," the Duke answered. "His efforts were lamentable, especially when he chose to bind some of our books in a hideous shade of orange leather. I remember my father having the greatest difficulty in not consigning them to the dustbin!"

Oletha had laughed. Then Harry had told a story of somebody who had decorated his house in a lime green that had made everybody who looked at it feel sea-sick.

She had not thought of what had been said until now.

Then suddenly it struck her that as the late Duke's friend had been a Classics scholar, would he not have chosen books that he personally appreciated on which to exercise his craft?

It was such a startling thought that without really thinking what she was doing Oletha sat up in bed.

A moment later she had turned on the light and was putting on her dressing-gown.

She knew it would be impossible to sleep

without ascertaining for herself if her idea was right and that the books which had seemed so elusive and which she had been seeking were not amongst the ancient volumes she had been inspecting, but because of their covers had been placed in a different part of the Library altogether.

She remembered what the Duke had said: that his father was not particularly interested in his books as his grandfather had been.

It all seemed to settle into a pattern: a classical scholar practising his skill as a book-binder on the most treasured volumes in the Gore collection; and his host, interested not in the contents but in the appearance of the volumes, banishing them to some obscure part of the Library where they had been forgotten.

"I must find out for certain—I must!" Oletha told herself.

She buttoned her dressing-gown down the front. It was a simple but very attractive gown of heavy blue crepe silk, trimmed with small rows of Valencian lace, threaded through with velvet ribbons and fastening with pearl buttons.

With her hair falling over it she looked very young and almost like an angel stepping down from the sky to bemuse mere mortals.

But Oletha was completely unconcerned with her appearance. She only wanted to know if her "hunch," her perceptive sense, was right and the book or books she sought were not where she had been looking ever since she had arrived at Gore, but in another part of the Library.

She opened the door of her bedroom to find that there were two lights left burning in the passage which made it easy for her to see her way.

As she descended the staircase to the first floor there were also lights burning in the Hall.

It was then she realised there was a nightwatchman seated in a padded leather chair with a covered top which stood just inside the front door.

Instead of walking down the Grand Staircase, she moved further along the wide corridor to where at the far end of it she knew was another staircase which she had seen near the Library.

There was no further sign of nightwatchmen, and having reached the foot of the staircase she went first to Mr. Hansard's office in search of the Library key.

When she had taken it to him, before going upstairs to dress for dinner, she had noticed without really thinking about it that he had put it not in one of the drawers of his desk, but in an engraved silver box which stood on top of it.

The office was in darkness, but as she had left the door open there was enough light from the passage for her to see the gleam of the silver box as she went into the room.

Picking it up she opened it, felt inside with her hand and her fingers encountered the key.

Then because she was impatient to prove her

theory right she hurried towards the Library, opening the door, and switching on a few of the lights as soon as she was inside.

It struck her again how vast the Library was and how it might take her hours to find, among the thousands of volumes, a few covered in orange leather.

Then she realised sensibly that because the Duke had disliked the way they had been bound he would have stored them out of sight, and had doubtless ordered that they be put on a top shelf which could only be reached by the balcony.

There was a tiny twisting brass staircase that led up to the balcony.

She climbed it and turned right towards the end of the room that was furthest from the door.

She had not had time since she arrived at Gore to inspect the balcony, and now she thought how skilfully it was designed. Even at a glance she could see that the shelves contained a large number of books which, if she had the time to read them, she would find extremely interesting.

But now she was in a hurry to find those she sought and some inner instinct told her where they would be.

Slowly she moved, her head tipped back, her eyes on the top shelf. Then with a leap of her heart she saw what she wanted to find.

Right against the ceiling at the far end where the balcony ended and a long window began there was a patch of orange that seemed at variance with the muted hues of the volumes around them.

Eagerly, feeling as if her fingers were trembling with excitement, Oletha drew out a book.

The cover was certainly a most unattractive colour and the binding was amateurish and badly executed.

At the same time that was quite unimportant. Oletha opened the book holding her breath, wondering what she would find.

For the moment, because she was so excited and so intensely interested, and also because it was not easy to see what she held in her hand, the writing seemed to dance before her eyes.

Then she saw that what she was looking at was the page of an ancient English Bible.

Hastily she turned to the front and found with a leap of her heart that it was the Geneva version of the Gospel of St. Matthew published by Christopher Baker in 1576!

She recognised it as being undoubtedly genuine and something which would delight the whole scholarly world and it certainly would, if he wished to sell it, bring the Duke a large sum of money.

She put it under her arm and reached up again to take down another book, and now as she opened it she knew incredibly that it was what she had been seeking.

She found herself looking at an engraving of

William Shakespeare on the title page of the First Folio Edition of his Plays, published in 1623!

"I have found it! I have found it!" Oletha wanted to cry aloud.

The rumours had been true and the treasure the Duke had longed for was here in her hands!

It was then as she looked in delight at the engraving of Shakespeare's bald head on the title page and his strangely shaped ruff, that she heard a sound and realised that it was footsteps approaching the Library.

She had not shut the door when she had entered, and she knew now she should have been sensible enough to lock herself in.

Swiftly, born of a sudden fear as to who was there, she pulled out a book from the bottom shelf and slipped first the Shakespeare Folio, then the Bible into the back of it.

There was just enough room for them, then as Oletha replaced the book she had moved, she knew without turning round that somebody had come into the Library and it was not the Duke.

With some instinct she could not explain but could not deny, she knew that whoever was interrupting her search constituted danger.

She moved swiftly along the balcony and only as she reached the steps in the centre of it did the man standing just inside the door and who had not moved since entering catch sight of her.

For a moment Harry Goring was still, then he

turned and shut the Library door behind him.

As he did so, Oletha began to descend the steps and by the time she had reached the floor he had walked down the room and was beside her.

"What are you doing here?" she enquired before he could speak.

"I rather expected you would be here," he replied. "I thought you would not miss the hint that my cousin gave you at dinner as to where the book we are seeking might be hidden."

"I . . . do not know what you are . . . talking about."

"You are a bad liar!" Harry Goring replied, "and now tell me what you have found."

"I have found . . . nothing!"

Despite a resolution to speak normally her voice trembled.

"You are lying!" Harry Goring said fiercely. "And as your partner I share your findings!"

"You are not my partner!" she retorted, "and as I have found nothing I intend to go back to bed and continue my search tomorrow."

She would have passed him, but he took a step so that he was standing squarely in front of her.

"Do you really think I accept that?" he asked. "I do not think you have been here long, and as you are in a hurry to leave, it is quite obvious that you have found the orange-bound volumes which the Duke mentioned."

"I am afraid your imagination is working overtime, Captain Goring," Oletha said in what she hoped was a scornful tone.

"If you have found the Folio, what have you done with it?" Harry Goring asked.

"Since you are determined not to believe anything I say to you, there is no point in my staying here," Oletha replied. "Goodnight, Captain Goring!"

She would have passed him but again he was in front of her, and now she thought there was an unpleasant smile on his lips.

"You really think you can trick me like this?" he asked. "I have offered you a present, but I presume you want money. Very well then, five per cent of what I get for the Folio."

"I thought your idea was that you should give the book, if it was found, to your cousin as a birthday present!" Oletha said scornfully.

"I was well aware that you did not believe me, so let us stop playing games," Harry Goring answered. "Show me where you have put it and, as I have already said, I will cut you in on the spoils. That is what you want, is it not?"

"Should I find something valuable here in this Library I shall hand it over to its rightful owner," Oletha replied, "who as you are well aware is the Duke."

She spoke defiantly. At the same time as she saw the expression on Harry Goring's face she was suddenly frightened.

Now he looked unpleasantly dangerous and she was aware how tall he was and that she was completely defenceless against him.

At the same time some pride would not permit her to show her fear. Instinctively her chin went up and her eyes as they defied him were definitely pansy-coloured.

"I think, Captain Goring, that you are completely despicable!" she said scathingly. "If you do not allow me to leave this room immediately I shall scream and the nightwatchman will come to my assistance."

Even when Harry Goring raised his arm she did not realise what he intended to do.

Then as he hit her across the side of her face so violently that she stumbled, she gave a little cry that seemed, from sheer shock, to be lost in her throat.

"Will you tell me where you have hidden the book, or do I have to beat it out of you?" Harry asked furiously.

As Oletha tried to regain her balance he hit her again, this time catching her on the side of her head so that she fell down on the floor.

Again she gave a little scream and knew as she did so, that it was too low and frightened to be heard outside the Library.

Harry Goring was towering over her.

"You will give in eventually," he said menacingly, "and you will find it a great deal less painful to do so now!"

It was not only what he said but the way he said it which told Oletha all too clearly that he would have no compunction about hitting her and continuing to hit her until out of sheer weakness she gave in to him.

Then as she thought despairingly that she was a coward and the pain he had already inflicted on her was almost unbearable, she heard the Library door open and a voice say furiously:

"What the hell do you think you are doing?"

For a moment Harry Goring was paralysed into immobility, then as if his crooked, agile brain grasped at a solution, he said:

"I am glad you have come, Sandor! I found this woman trying to steal the Shakespeare folio which she has found and hidden!"

"An interesting explanation!" the Duke said and his voice was like a whip. "I do not believe it and I will not allow a guest in my house to be treated in this manner. For your own good Harry, you had better leave me—now."

There was a moment's pause, then Harry said with an attempt at a jaunty air:

"Well, of course, if that is what you wish! But I warn you not to trust her, and not to listen to her lies."

The Duke said nothing. He merely stood looking at his cousin. Harry, as if he knew he was beaten, walked away and leaving the Library slammed the door to behind him.

The Duke waited until he was quite certain he

had gone, then he went down on one knee and put his arms around Oletha.

Because she was so shocked by what had occurred, and at the same time, utterly relieved because he had saved her, she gave an inarticulate little murmur and hid her face against his shoulder.

He held her against him, then rose slowly to his feet, lifting her to hers, but keeping his arms closely around her.

"What happened?" he asked. "I was going riding because I could not sleep, when I heard you scream."

He could feel she was trembling and knew that for the moment it was impossible for her to speak.

Very gently he put his hand under her chin and turned her face up to his so that he could look at her.

It was then he saw the crimson mark on her cheek where Harry had hit her.

He stared it at incredulously. Then he saw the joy in her face because he was there, before tears began to run down her cheeks.

"You are all right," the Duke said gently. "He shall not hurt you again."

Then, almost as if he could not help himself, his lips came down on hers.

For a moment Oletha could hardly believe it was happening. Then she knew that from what had been a hell of fear, she had been lifted into a Heaven of happiness she had not even known existed.

As the Duke took possession of her lips she realised that this was what she had been wanting and longing for from the moment she had come to Gore, and she knew now that she had fallen in love with him the moment she had seen him.

Every time he spoke to her, every time he came close to her, she had been acutely conscious of him and her whole being had vibrated towards him in a manner which only because she was so ignorant, she had not realised was love.

But it was love, and he awakened her to the wonder of it as his mouth held hers captive, and she felt as if she was no longer herself but his and he filled the whole world.

It was impossible to think or try or understand what was happening. She was only aware that her whole body vibrated to something so perfect, so wonderful that it was like celestial music in her ears.

She felt the Duke's arms tighten and now his lips that had been gentle became insistent and demanding, and she thought he had in fact taken complete possession of her and there was nothing she could do but give him what he wanted.

"My darling, my sweet!" he said. "I have fought against this from the moment I saw you."

"Did you . . . really feel . . . like . . . that?" Oletha questioned, but her voice was almost inaudible.

"When I came into this room and first saw you," the Duke said, "I thought you were the most beautiful thing I had ever seen in my life."

"And . . . then?"

"I knew I had found at last what I had always been seeking but had expected never to find. Then there you were, looking exactly as you do now, so perfect and so different from anyone I had ever seen before."

"That . . . was how I . . . felt about you."

"I am different!" the Duke said firmly. "I am different now in that you belong to me. You are mine! I have never been so sure of anything in my whole life!"

Then he was kissing her again, kissing her possessively and passionately and her whole body was trembling not with fear but with an ecstasy that seemed to run through her veins.

It made her feel as if she had suddenly come alive in a way she had never been alive before. . . .

"I . . . love . . . you!" she said a long while later, when she could feel the Duke's heart beating against hers.

He did not answer, but merely picked her up in his arms and carried her to a sofa by the dying fire.

He sat down, cradling her against him almost as if she was a baby, and his lips were on the softness of her skin, moving over her bruised cheek, then kissing her eyes, her small straight nose, then again her lips.

"I love you!" he said in his deep voice. "I adore you, and I know now I have never wanted anything as much as I want you."

"This . . . cannot be happening," Oletha whispered.

"Why not?" the Duke enquired. "We might have known that in some strange way Fate would shape us to her own ends and there was nothing we could do about it."

"Would you have . . . wished to . . . prevent it?" Oletha asked in a small voice.

"The only thing that matters in the whole world is you," he replied.

Then he was kissing her again, kissing her until she could feel the fire rising within him, touching his lips and an answering flame in her breast rose in her.

His kisses intensified and because she was just a little afraid she put up her hands in protest and the Duke raised his head.

"Have I frightened you, my darling?" he asked. "It is something I do not wish to do, but I cannot begin to tell you what you mean to me. It is all a strange, unaccountable magic for which I have no explanation."

"I am . . . glad . . . so very glad!" Oletha murmured. "I did not know that kisses could be so wonderful . . . or so glorious!"

"You have never been kissed before?"

She smiled and shook her head.

"Oh, my darling, I was meant to be the first

in your life, just as I was meant to be the man to whom you would belong."

He paused before he added:

"I have lived in the East too long not to know that this is not the first time we have met. It is not the first time I have seen your lovely face, your strange pansy-coloured eyes. From that first moment in the Library they have haunted me, and I know now I can never be free of them."

The way he spoke gave Oletha a strange sensation that left her breathless.

"I love . . . you!" she said, "but I . . . think perhaps now . . . I should to go bed."

"Yes, of course," the Duke agreed, "but it is hard for me to let you go."

He took his arms from her and as she sat upright on the sofa he said:

"We will talk again tomorrow, but we have all our lives in front of us."

The way he spoke made her thrill and Oletha put her head against his shoulder with a little gesture that was instinctively caressing.

She felt his lips against her forehead, then he rose to his feet.

"I must not tire you, my precious one," he said. "I must send you to bed and make sure that my despicable cousin leaves first thing in the morning, before you have to see him again."

He paused. Then as if he suddenly thought of it, he asked:

"Have you found anything? Were you really

hiding something from him?"

"I was hiding it for . . . you," Oletha replied. "I have found the Shakespeare First Folio and the Geneva Bible and I know both are extremely valuable!"

"You have really found them?" the Duke asked. "Oh, my precious, this makes everything so much easier than it would have been otherwise."

She knew only too well what he was saying, but because she had to know for certain, she asked:

"You . . . mean that you can . . . spend the money on . . . Gore?"

"I mean that I can marry you without feeling I am being selfish," the Duke replied.

He smiled at her before he added:

"It was what I intended to do whatever the consequences, but if you have really found something valuable, then, as I say, it will make things very much easier."

"They are worth a lot of money," Oletha said reassuringly, "and there may be other . . . books as well."

She had a strange feeling as she spoke that the Duke was not listening.

He was looking at her and the expression in his eyes made her feel shy.

"I love you, and I want you!" he said. "How soon can we be married? I presume we have to ask your father?"

It was then Oletha realised that she had a great deal of explaining to do and was not certain how she could do so.

Because she felt bemused she said quickly:

"Let me show you . . . where the books are, and I think you should . . . take them with you to your . . . bedroom."

"Of course!" the Duke agreed.

He still spoke absently, and his eyes were on her lips.

Then abruptly he pulled her against him and was kissing her fiercely, passionately, demandingly, as if he was afraid he might lose her.

Chapter Six

TRAVELLING BY train to London Oletha thought that in a way she had been very clever.

Having never done anything for herself before, she felt it must be her American blood which made her so efficient in an emergency.

When she had left the Duke and gone to bed last night, she had felt as if it was impossible to think; she could only feel that she was in a magical world which enveloped her like a rainbow, and her heart as well as her eyes were dazzled by the wonder of it.

She had known he felt the same because when she put the two books she had discovered into his hands, he had hardly glanced at them. Instead his eyes were on her lips and she felt as if he was still kissing her.

"We will talk about everything tomorrow," he had said almost mechanically, and she knew it was as hard for him to let her go as it was for her to leave.

It was only as they walked with their arms entwined towards the Library door that she remembered she was wearing a dressing-gown and that she must not be seen by the footmen on duty in the Hall.

Because they were so closely attuned to each other he knew before she spoke, what she was thinking.

He gave her a smile as he said:

"You look very lovely, my darling, and your hair is an enchantment that has cast a spell over me from which I can never escape. At the same time, I have no wish for anyone to see you like this, except myself."

The note of passion in his voice made her quiver, and as she looked up at him and their eyes met, neither of them moved.

"I must . . . leave you," she murmured at last.

"Only for a very short time," he answered. "Tomorrow we will make plans as to when we can be married and after that you will never leave me, my darling one."

Because she was almost afraid of the sensations he aroused in her, Oletha said in a voice he could hardly hear:

"I . . . must go now . . . and please . . . please be careful of the books."

Without looking back she ran away down the passage towards the staircase, appearing in her blue gown almost like a ghost.

Only when the shadows had swallowed her up and she was completely out of sight, did the Duke give a deep sigh and turn back into the Library to put out the lights and lock the door behind him.

When she reached her bedroom Oletha threw herself down on her bed just as she was and lay there for a long time feeling a wild inexpressible happiness sweep over her.

Yet she forced herself to remember that soon she had to tell the Duke the truth about herself, and wondered how best she could do so.

Finally, when she took off her dressing-gown and got into bed, she had come to the conclusion that she must first go home to prevent Mr. Baron from arriving before she and her father did.

'It is not going to be easy,' she thought.

The conviction that it was, in fact, going to be very, very difficult was now almost like a menacing cloud as the milk-train chugged its way slowly towards London.

She had discovered by consulting the printed time-table on the desk in her bedroom the time at which the train stopped at the station for Gore.

She had known that unless she was prepared to make explanations to the Duke which she felt were impossible, she must leave before he awoke.

It was just before four o'clock in the morning when she rang the bell and after some delay the maid who looked after her hurried into her bedroom.

"Are you ill, Miss?" she asked breathlessly.

She was staring in astonishment at Oletha who was already half-dressed and had one of her trunks open in which she was packing her gowns.

"No, I am not ill," Oletha replied, "but I have to leave immediately for London and I see there is a train at ten minutes to five which I intend to catch."

There was a rush which fortunately left no time for her to answer any questions, or for the maid to inform the Housekeeper or, worse still, Mr. Hansard.

Anyway, Oletha knew, they would not think she was important enough for it to be of any momentous concern that she was leaving earlier than any guest at Gore was expected to do.

The carriage which conveyed her to the station only had a coachman on the box which conveniently left room for her trunks. At the same time, it was definitely an indication that her social status was not very high in the servants' estimation.

Now she was on her way home Oletha felt it had been quite an achievement to get as far as London.

When the train reached Paddington she told a porter to collect her trunks from the Guard's Van and he procured her a hackney-carriage that took her to the small house occupied by her Nanny where Martha was staying.

The two old women had just finished their breakfast when Oletha appeared, and Martha was extremely surprised to see her.

"Miss Oletha!" she cried. "Whatever are you doing here at this hour of the morning? And why in a hired cab, of all things?"

"I will explain on the way home," Oletha replied, "but now I want to say 'Hello' to Nanny and tell her how glad I am to see her."

She kissed her old Nurse who exclaimed at her appearance and said how pretty she had become.

By the time Oletha had accepted a cup of tea and Martha had hurried up the narrow stairs to collect her belongings there was no opportunity to explain her early arrival or why she had not travelled, as she would have expected, in one of the carriages belonging to the Graysons.

It was only when they set off for home that Martha more or less demanded to be told what had been happening.

"I want you to help me, Martha," Oletha said, "and it is something you have always been willing to do in the past."

"I'm not doing anything your father wouldn't approve of, Miss Oletha, as you well know," Martha replied.

Then her curiosity overcame her and she asked:

"Tell me what you wants."

"First I want you to promise not to tell Papa I have been to London," Oletha replied, "but if he hears of it from Mr. Allen, as he may, then please do not say you have been staying with Nanny."

"Now what's going on?" Martha enquired. "I don't like it, and that's the truth. I thought it was strange when you told me in the first place that I was not to stay with you at Her Ladyship's."

"Oh, please, Martha, do not ask a lot of questions," Oletha pleaded. "I am tired and worried, and to tell you the truth I have a headache."

She shut her eyes as she spoke and because Martha was genuinely fond of her, she knew that the old maid would for the moment in her concern not press her to say any more.

Only when she was back in her familiar surroundings did Oletha feel as if she had stepped out of a dream into reality.

Had she really been to Gore in such a strange manner and managed to be such a good actress that the Duke had believed her to be the daughter of a Curator?

And yet, because their love for each other was irresistible and so overwhelming, he had actually asked her to be his wife.

She told herself that if she had read the story in a book she would never have believed it for a moment.

Dukes, of all men, did not marry impulsively and for love. As her father had said, marriages for the aristocracy were a business arrangement and both parties benefited financially from a union.

But the Duke was different.

He loved her and while she was certain that in such circumstances another man of his rank would have suggested a very different position for her in his life, he had offered her marriage.

"I love him! I love him!" she said to herself a thousand times. "Could any man be so wonderful?"

It was a rapture that was almost inexpressible to know that she had found, as her mother had, a man who captured her heart from the moment she saw him and loved her for herself and not for her money.

Her father had been wrong; love at first sight did happen, not once in a million times but for the second time in her family in two generations.

She felt almost as if her mother was standing beside her.

"I have found him, Mama. I have found him!" Oletha said, "and he loves me, the real me! My money does not matter!"

Her heart was singing and she thought it was the same music she had heard when the Duke had kissed her and was a melody which came from the skies.

She was thinking of him every second of the

day as she wandered around the house, unable to settle down to do anything but remember the strength of his arms and the touch of his lips on hers.

She talked to Mr. Baron and made him agree that he would not go to Gore before the Monday after the shooting party.

"You make me very apprehensive of the reception I will receive, Miss Ashurst," Mr. Baron said warily.

"There is nothing to worry about," Oletha replied confidently. "By the time you arrive all the explanations will be over. I shall have made them, and when you see the Library you will forget everything else."

She told him how she had found the Shakespeare Folio and the Geneva Bible and he was astonished.

"Are you sure they are genuine, Miss Ashurst?"

"Absolutely sure!" Oletha replied.

She told him how they had been bound in the old Duke's time by a Professor from Oxford and Mr. Baron agreed it was unlikely he would have troubled to bind fakes.

"What do you think they will be worth when the Duke sells them?" she asked.

"Sells them!" Mr. Baron exclaimed in horror. "Surely His Grace is not contemplating despoiling the Library at Gore of what must be its finest and most precious treasures?"

Oletha felt embarrassed.

She had spoken without thinking, and now she felt she should not have disclosed the Duke's private affairs even to Mr. Baron.

"Please do not mention it to His Grace," she said a little uncomfortably, "but he is extremely hard up and he is very anxious to pay off some of the debts incurred by the late Duke and to do some very necessary repairs to the house."

"It would be a crime, a real crime, for the collection I expect to find at Gore to be broken up," Mr. Baron protested.

Oletha did not know what to say. She could only make him promise not to disclose anything she had said to him.

She wondered how many people would bring pressure on the Duke not to dispose of the books now they had been found.

Then she thought if he did sell them it would be quite easy for her Trustees to buy them back on her behalf. Of course they would have to tell her father.

All the same ever since she arrived home Oletha, having seen the Duke, had known, just as her father did, that he was the last man on earth who would wish to be labelled a fortune-hunter.

It suddenly struck her that, instead of being unconcerned by learning that the woman he wanted to marry was not a poor Curator's daughter but an immensely rich heiress, he might resent it.

Almost as if someone had thrown a bucket of

156

cold water over her she found herself remembering how her father had said that "no decent Englishman" would ever ask her to marry him.

She could hear his voice saying it gravely, and yet with an unmistakable ring of sincerity.

"No decent Englishman."

Was that how the Duke would feel?

She felt a stab of fear in her heart that was physically painful.

Supposing ... supposing, she asked herself, the Duke, having enough money now for his immediate needs, refused to marry her because she was wealthy?

It seemed improbable, in fact incredible, that he should do so, and yet the fear within Oletha seemed to grow and multiply until it menaced her like a heavy storm on the horizon which drew nearer and nearer.

"What will he say?" she asked, and remembered that it was not her love that was being put to the test, but his.

"It will be all right, of course," she told herself over and over again.

Then she remembered how her father had said he would never have married her mother if she had been as rich then as she became eventually.

She had thought at the time he was exaggerating. Her father and mother had loved each other so completely that it was impossible to think of their ever being married to anybody else but each other.

And yet her father was very proud, and she

remembered how careful her mother had been never to say or suggest in any way that her money provided anything they needed.

Oletha felt she could not stay still. Perturbed by her thoughts she walked about restlessly and when she went to bed she could not sleep.

It was only just before her father arrived the next day that she suddenly came to a decision.

She decided, although she had not formulated it completely in her mind, that because the Duke was in love with her and she with him, she would tell him the truth.

He would be angry, very angry, at her behaving in such an unconventional manner, but she felt certain she could persuade him that the end had justified the means.

She and the Duke were in love and there would be no question of their not being marvellously happy.

She knew, because she and her father were so close, that he had in fact been afraid that she would oppose him and either refuse to go to Gore or else make it impossible once she got there for the Duke to ask her to be his wife.

She was quite certain that her father was prepared to overrule her and force her to do as he wished, but it would certainly make things very much easier if she was not only willing to marry the Duke but absolutely determined to do so.

'Love is more important than anything else,' she thought consolingly, and told herself she was sure the Duke would feel the same.

The doubt however, persisted, and when her father stepped from the carriage to kiss her affectionately he said:

"You look worried, my darling. What has happened?"

She knew then she could not tell him.

"N–nothing, Papa," she answered. "I have just been longing to see you."

The die was cast. She had lied and now she must go on pretending that nothing had occurred while he had been away, and must leave all the explanations until they reached Gore.

Fortunately her father's thoughts were concentrated on their visit and he had no wish to talk of anything else.

"I do not believe any man in the world could have produced a finer collection of gowns than I have bought in so short a time," he boasted. "And I thought, Oletha, you might like to wear some of your mother's jewellery, so I have brought some of it from the Bank where I had left it in safe-keeping."

As if he noticed that Oletha was somewhat unresponsive, he went on:

"You cannot of course, wear her large or more valuable jewels, but I have brought a collection of diamonds which, with its unique stones, will look very lovely around your long neck, and the turquoise set which I think is particularly attractive for a young girl."

The word "turquoise" made Oletha think of Harry Goring and the way he had tried to bribe her with turquoises.

She was quite certain that if she had handed over the folio to him she would never have seen the jewels, but because she felt that he had somehow spoilt the beauty of them for her, she said quickly:

"I think it would be a mistake, Papa, for me to wear jewels which other girls of my age would not possess. I would not wish the . . . D–Duke or his guests to think I was parading my wealth."

Her voice quivered when she mentioned the Duke, but her father did not notice.

"Perhaps you are right," the Colonel said, "and like your mother you are sensitive to other people's feelings. Wear your pearls as usual, but we will take the other jewels with us just in case you need them."

"Yes, of course, Papa," Oletha said meekly.

Because she knew it would please him she inspected the clothes he had bought for her. The hats were certainly more sophisticated than anything she had worn before.

The one in which she was to travel was trimmed with ostrich feathers and the thick felt one she was to wear out shooting was ornamented with several quills. It was very smart and as her father told her the very latest vogue from Paris.

"Just as I thought," Martha said, determined to find fault. "Your father didn't remember the accessories you'd need, but I bought you some new gloves, Miss Oletha, and several pairs of evening slippers, besides a pair of buttoned boots in which you can go shooting."

"I knew you would remember everything, Martha," Oletha smiled, "but be careful not to mention in front of Papa that you have been to London. He would be very upset if he thought he had forgotten anything that was really essential."

They set off early the following morning, and as usual travelled in the comfort that Mr. Allan arranged so efficiently, but it was nothing to the luxury that was waiting for them at Paddington.

Oletha did not know that the 4th Duke of Gorleston had copied, as most other noblemen did, the way His Royal Highness conveyed his guests to Sandringham.

She was therefore astonished, while her father had expected it, to find the Duke's private train waiting for them at the station.

There were servants wearing the Gore livery to greet them as soon as they stepped out of their carriage, and other servants to attend to their luggage.

Oletha had a quick glance at the baggage for Gore that stood near the Guard's Van, and thought it seemed like a small mountain.

She was not aware that when the Prince was present no lady would be seen wearing the same clothes more than once, which meant that even for a visit of two or three days an astronomical amount of luggage was necessary.

There were a number of extremely elegant guests now proceeding towards the private train and her father appeared to know them all.

"No need to ask why you are coming, Ashurst," Oletha heard one of the gentlemen say. "There is an unpleasant rumour going around that the new Duke intends to dispose of his father's stable. That is something you must prevent at all costs."

Colonel Ashurst smiled enigmatically, but his friend persisted:

"I hope it is only a rumor. We cannot afford to lose the old and respected owners to the sharp financiers who are now taking to the Sport of Kings."

There was an obvious innuendo in what he said, and several people who were standing near to him laughed.

"I am sure Colonel Ashurst, who knows more about horses than anybody else in the country, will show the Duke where his duty lies," a very beautiful woman said. "And that is to carry on the Goring tradition, is it not, Colonel?"

Oletha noticed she smiled at her father admiringly and thought it was not surprising as he was an extremely handsome and attractive man.

It was only when he had introduced her as his daughter that she noticed a different expression on his friends' faces and a sudden alertness which told her they were aware how rich she was and guessed the reason why she was included in the party.

Oletha felt so embarrassed that she wanted to run away and hide.

"The Duke is not marrying me for my money!" she longed to shout.

But she felt already they were beginning to spoil something so beautiful and so magical that like fairy gold it would vanish at the touch of human fingers.

After they were seated in the train somebody asked:

"What is the delay?"

A steward who was handing round the champagne explained:

"We're waiting for His Royal Highness, M'Lady."

"He is coming with us?"

"In the same train, M'Lady, but His Royal Highness has a private coach to himself."

A gentleman laughed.

"I thought he would not miss the first shoot of the Season at Gore."

"Who would want to do that, considering the bag we got last time?" another guest replied.

They all began to talk of the previous year's shoot and the enormous number of pheasants that had been shot.

Because Oletha not only enjoyed shooting herself but always studied the game returns from the shoots her father attended, she knew that over two thousand had been killed in one day and they were all exceptionally high birds.

"I sincerely hope Gorleston is not thinking of economising on his shoots!" someone exclaimed. "The Prince has always said he would rather shoot at Gore than almost any other place he knows."

"Perhaps it is a question of a choice between the horses and the pheasants," an elderly man suggested.

"Good Lord! Are you suggesting it must be one or the other?"

"Apparently the late Duke left a pile of debts."

There was silence for a moment. Then one of the ladies exclaimed:

"I cannot bear to think we might no longer enjoy our lovely visits to Gore. We have always had such fun in that magnificent house. And Charlie says if the furnishings are shabby the cellar is not!"

Everyone laughed. Then another man sitting on the other side of the carriage remarked:

"Well, the new Duke is young and healthy, and my wife tells me extremely good-looking. All he wants is a wife with money, and that should not be hard to find."

For a moment there was that uncomfortable silence when people realise that someone has made a gaffe.

Then everybody began to talk at once.

Oletha, looking out of the window, saw the Prince of Wales attended by a large number of servants, board the train and then they set off at once.

She had left the station at Gore yesterday morning when it was still dark. Now there was a red carpet on the platform. The Prince alighted first and was carried away in a carriage drawn by four horses.

Gore was looking more magnificent and more impressive Oletha thought, than it had been when she had last seen it, and now it seemed over-powering.

She felt that she was growing smaller and smaller until like Alice in Wonderland everything around her was over-large and she could hardly be seen at all.

She wondered if her father had any idea what she was feeling and she wished now she had told him the truth.

He would have understood that she was not really embarrassed by Gore and all the fashionable guests, but at seeing the Duke again.

Would he look at her with that light in his eyes and a gladness that seemed to illuminate his face and made her heart beat frantically?

'He loves me and because I love him it will be all right,' she thought.

She told herself consolingly that at least she

was looking much more beautiful than she had ever done before.

Her new travelling-gown accentuated her slim figure, and her sable-trimmed cloak completed an expensive ensemble unrivalled by any other lady in the party.

Still Oletha was afraid as the horses turned in at the lodge gates, and she began to wonder what she would say if, when they arrived, the Duke exclaimed: "Miss Baron—I was not expecting you!"

She had left him a note on her dressing-table, which she knew he would receive at breakfast-time, saying that she would go away for a short time.

She had written:

"I have to go, and I will explain why when I see you again, which will be very, very shortly. Forgive me for not telling you last evening, but I will be with you again as quickly as possible. I love you."

She signed the letter "Oletha" and told herself as she did so that in the future she would never lie to him. He would understand why she had come to Gore pretending to be someone else, so that she could find out what sort of man he was.

'I did find out and he is wonderful!' she thought.

She was certain they could never have felt the same about each other if she had not been brave enough to behave in what her father would consider a very reprehensible manner.

"The Duke will understand. He will know that I was seeking the truth because I wanted love— the real love which I have found," Oletha told herself.

Yet as she walked up the steps and into the huge marble hall she was aware that she was trembling.

Her father had told her that the Duke would greet them immediately on their arrival before they went to their rooms.

But there was no sign of him and Mr. Hansard came forward to say:

"His Grace begs you to excuse him for not welcoming you as he planned to do, but His Royal Highness wished to have a private word with him, and he felt sure you would understand."

"Yes, of course!" the ladies in the party murmured.

Then everybody was proceeding upstairs and Oletha found herself in a much grander bedroom than the one which she had occupied on the second floor.

There was a different maid to help Martha unpack for her, and she felt as if the moment of confrontation had passed at least for another hour or so.

Her father was in the next room, and later when she had bathed and changed into one of her new gowns, he came to escort her downstairs for dinner.

"What are you wearing?" he asked as he came into the room. "As I have often told you before, Oletha, first impressions are very important."

Oletha gave a little smile, thinking of the moment when she and the Duke had first met and how he had said it was then that he had fallen in love with her.

"I thought this was the prettiest of the gowns you bought for me, Papa," she replied.

It was certainly very lovely with a full skirt of white tulle, and at the same time very different from the ordinary white gown of a debutante. It had tiny diamante glittering from waist to hem and more diamante-like tear-drops around the shoulders and on the small puffed sleeves.

It was a young girl's gown, and yet it had a sophistication that only money could achieve, and Colonel Ashurst noted with approval that Oletha was wearing the collet of diamonds around her throat.

She wore them almost as a weapon with which to defend herself, and yet she felt nothing could really give her the confidence she needed.

"Are you ready?" her father was asking. "We must not be late the first evening, which is usually very formal, and we all have to be down before the Prince of Wales."

"Is Princess Alexandra with him?" Oletha asked.

"No, Mrs. Keppel is, which means he will be in a good humour," her father replied.

He smiled as he added:

"And so he ought to be. Most of His Royal Highness's closest friends are present, and as they happen to be the best game-shots in the country, I imagine the Duke will make every effort to see that we get a record number of birds."

Oletha did not say anything, but she felt the Duke was thinking that it was perhaps his "swan-song." If he could no longer afford the shoots at Gore, at least he would see they went out with a "bang."

The money he would get from the sale of the books she had discovered for him might be enough for the more urgent repairs to the house and for the pensions, but she was sure he would be planning to curtail the racing and shooting on which his father had spent thousands of pounds every year.

'In a few minutes,' she thought, 'he will know that he can have everything he wants . . . and love!'

She felt herself quiver at the idea and she wished she had been brave enough to go downstairs after they had arrived and asked if she could see the Duke alone.

She thought that was what she might have done had he not been with the Prince, in which case she would merely have been told politely to go away.

As she and her father walked slowly down the Grand Staircase she had the uncomfortable feeling that she was moving towards a situation which might prove disastrous.

Supposing the Duke was so surprised at her appearance that he accused her of deceiving him in front of her father and his other guests?

Supposing he denounced her as an imposter, telling everybody that she had wormed her way into Gore under false pretences?

This was something she was well aware he would never do, and yet she frightened herself with the idea.

There were two people in front of them and now they stopped in front of a pair of large double doors where there were two footmen wearing powdered wigs in attendance and a Major Domo.

She heard the latter announce the guests as they entered the Salon:

"The Marquess and Marchioness of Ripon, Your Grace!"

For a moment Oletha wondered where she had heard the name, then remembered her father telling her that the Marquess was one of the finest shots in England.

They reached the door while the Duke was still greeting the Marquess and his beautiful wife, and the Major Domo paused before he announced them.

Oletha looked at the Duke and felt her heart turn over in her breast.

She had thought he looked magnificent when she had dined alone with him and Harry Goring, but now, wearing, because the Prince of Wales was present, his decorations, she felt suddenly as if he was someone different altogether and too important for her to have any real contact with.

A sudden panic swept over her and she felt the only thing in life that mattered had slipped through her fingers before she could even hold onto it.

This was not the man who had held her in his arms and told her that she was his and he could not live without her. This was not the man who had kissed her until she felt as if they were disembodied, that their feet were no longer on the ground and they touched the stars.

This was somebody as far removed from reality and herself as if he were the Prince of Wales himself.

"Colonel Ashurst, Your Grace, and Miss Ashurst!" the Major Domo boomed.

Now they were walking forward, moving towards the Duke, and Oletha felt as if her heart was beating so suffocatingly that everybody must hear it.

The Duke's face seemed to swim before her eyes, then she heard his voice.

"How are you, Colonel? Delighted to welcome you to Gore! I hope we shall get a good bag tomorrow."

"There is no doubt about that," the Colonel replied. "Was not that why you invited us here?"

"I think you invited yourselves," the Duke said with a laugh. "You all know more about the shoot than I do, having been unable to participate for the last seven years."

"You will soon catch up," Colonel Ashurst joked.

Then as if he suddenly remembered Oletha's presence he said:

"May I introduce my daughter? This is her first big house-party and I am sure she will find it an unforgettable experience."

Oletha held her breath.

Then almost as if she was a puppet with her father pulling the strings she put out her hand and dropped a small curtsy.

"I am delighted that you should have your first house-party here at Gore," the Duke said, "and I hope it will not prove to be a disappointment."

As he spoke Oletha raised her eyes to look up at him, knowing she was holding out her hand almost as if he would save her from drowning in her own fears.

Then as she looked at him she realised, incredibly, unbelievably, that there was not a flicker of recognition in his face.

Only, she thought, grimness which had swept the smile from his lips.

Chapter Seven

"I HAVE lost him!" Oletha told herself, "I have lost him!"

She saw the Duke laughing and talking with his friends and was aware that he had not once looked at her since the first moment she had arrived.

She had at first been so stunned by the fact that he appeared not to recognise her that she walked into the Salon as if she was in a dream, and it was impossible to think of what she should say or what she was doing.

How could it be possible that after all he had said, after he had told her she was his for all eternity, that he could fail to recognise her or could deliberately treat her as if she was a stranger he had never seen before?

174

Then as she moved further down the Salon with her father to where there was a group of people he wished to meet, she recognised one of them.

"How delightful to see you, Oletha dear!" Lady Grayson said. "I have just been talking to our host and telling him that I have known you ever since you were born."

So that, Oletha knew, was how the Duke was prepared for her arrival.

For the rest of the evening he did not once look in her direction nor make any effort to speak to her.

He even somehow contrived not to say good-night to her, and as she cried helplessly on her pillow in the darkness of her bedroom she knew that her dreams had fallen about her ears.

Now there was no urgent reason for him to marry her for her money. She was no longer of interest to him either as the woman he loved or as an heiress.

Despite her misery she went down to breakfast feeling that perhaps the morning would bring a change of heart and the Duke would at least ask her to give him an explanation as to why she had come to Gore under false pretences.

But he was not in the Breakfast-Room although everybody else was present, even the older ladies who were determined to watch the shooting.

It was a perfect day with a clear sky and just

a touch of frost to make everything, even the air, seem to sparkle.

But as the day progressed it might, as far as Oletha was concerned, have been shrouded in the thickest fog.

Now she saw the Duke differently from how she had seen him before—as the perfect host!

She was aware that he had told his keepers to arrange the Shoot as it had been in the past, but he was also making amendments and improving the positions of the guns, especially that of the Prince.

It was obvious that His Royal Highness was enjoying himself.

Last night at dinner Oletha had noticed that he was laughing at everything the two attractive ladies on either side of him said, and there was no sign of his well-known warning signal of boredom—the drumming of his fingers on the table.

Now he had had a good morning's sport and after luncheon was looking forward to three more drives.

On the first two there were as many birds as any gun could hope for, but the last, her father told Oletha, was a test of even the most experienced game-shot.

"I have never seen higher birds anywhere," the Colonel said with relish, "and I am in a very good place."

They had all drawn for position before the day

started with the exception of the Prince, who was placed in what was considered the best stand for every drive.

It was a short walk towards the wood and Colonel Ashurst was at one corner of it.

To reach his place he and Oletha had to walk down a ride cut between the trees and she saw there was a stand in the centre of it.

"That is where our host will be," Colonel Ashurst said as they passed, "and the birds are so high at this particular spot that we shall know when the drive is over whether he is as good a marksman as his father was."

They walked on and the Colonel found the stick which marked his position. His loader loaded his first gun, handed it to him, then loaded the second.

A bird came over but although the Colonel raised his gun, it was really out of shot and he did not fire.

Then the loader said:

"Excuse me, Sir. I'm afraid we're rather short of cartridges. I didn't notice it until now."

The Colonel frowned.

"That was careless of you!" he snapped. "I have been in this stand before and I expect to have a lot of shooting."

"I'm sorry, Sir," the loader said. "Shall I ask His Grace if he could spare some?"

The Colonel hesitated, then he said:

"You go and tell the Duke what has happened, Oletha. I do not want to be left with only one gun when the birds begin to come over."

"No, of course not, Papa."

Oletha retraced her steps around the wood and saw that the Duke was now in position in the centre of the ride, standing back against the trees with a gun in his hand, his loader just behind him.

He did not see her as she approached, but when she reached his side he turned his head to look at her, then quickly turned away again.

For a moment it was almost impossible for Oletha to find her voice. Then she said breathlessly:

"Papa says . . . could you be very . . . kind and let him have some . . . cartridges? He is . . . afraid he will not have . . . enough."

"Yes, of course," the Duke answered coldly.

He turned to the loader behind him.

"Take Colonel Ashurst my second bag, Barton," he ordered.

The loader propped the Duke's second gun carefully against a tree then picking up a bag of cartridges walked quickly away.

Oletha did not move. She knew this was the moment she had been waiting for when she was alone with the Duke and had a chance to speak to him.

And yet it was very difficult to know where to begin.

Once again he was not looking at her, but staring at the wood ahead.

"Please . . . let me tell . . ." she began in a very small voice.

As she spoke a high pheasant came over the trees in front of the Duke and he put up his gun and fired at it.

It was moving very fast and Oletha thought he had missed it, then she thought she heard a sound behind her and turned to see if the bird had carried on only to fall into the wood at their back.

As she did so she saw to her astonishment a little way back, the barrel of a gun poking out from some thick bushes.

She thought it was strange. Then as the Duke beside her raised his gun at another pheasant even higher than the first Oletha was suddenly aware that the gun hidden in the bushes was pointed at him!

Without thinking, without even considering what she should do, she hurled herself against the Duke and because he was bending backwards to fire at the bird overhead he stumbled and half-fell to the ground with Oletha on top of him.

At the same moment there was an explosion that seemed almost to break her ear-drums.

She felt pellets thudding against her hat and her fur-lined cape, then there was an agony in her neck which made her scream.

"You are a very lucky young woman!" the Doctor said, as he applied some lint to Oletha's neck. "Your maid tells me there were dozens of pellets in your cape and hat which fortunately did not penetrate any further."

"Three were painful enough!" Oletha said a little wryly.

"I can quite believe it," the Doctor said, "but I cannot understand anyone using such a large bore for pheasant-shooting."

He looked down at one of the pellets that he had just removed from her neck. Then he said in a different voice:

"If a whole cartridge of them had hit a man's head that was unprotected it could have been very serious."

"You . . . mean!" Oletha said with a little tremor in her voice: "that it could . . . kill a . . . man?"

"A wound in the head is always dangerous," the Doctor answered, "because of the damage it does to the brain."

Oletha drew in her breath.

She knew now who had fired the gun she had seen in the bushes and she knew from whom she had saved the Duke.

"This is the first time there has been a shooting accident at Gore for years," the Doctor was saying. "It is unfortunate it should happen at His Grace's first shoot, but luckily little damage has been done."

He smiled at Oletha as if he wished to apologise for minimising the pain she suffered and went on:

"You were well protected and that undoubtedly prevented it from being much more serious than it might otherwise have been. An accident with a shot-gun has often proved to be lethal."

Oletha understood from what the Doctor was saying what explanation the Duke had given of what had occurred.

When he had picked her up in his arms and carried her to the shooting-brake that was waiting to take the guns back to Gore, she had been too shocked and in too much pain to speak.

It had nevertheless, been an inexpressible comfort to feel herself close against him and most of all to know that he was safe.

Safe, she thought now, from his diabolical and wicked cousin who, having failed to steal from him, was now prepared to murder him.

"Now rest quietly," the Doctor was saying, "and if you take my advice, Miss Ashurst, you will miss the dance which I understand is taking place tonight. Have a quiet dinner here in your Sitting-Room or, better still, in bed."

He looked at her kindly and added:

"I know it is hard at your age not to be the Belle of the Ball, but your neck will be painful for the next twenty-four hours, and being shot at, even accidentally, is always a shock to the system."

He picked up his bag, then as he walked towards the door, he added:

"If you disregard my advice, as I expect you will, then try to rest tomorrow. I will call during the morning to make sure there is no inflammation from where I have removed the pellets."

"Thank you," Oletha said.

He left her and she could hear his voice outside the door giving instructions to Martha who was making far more fuss than she was about the accident.

Oletha lay back against the cushions of the *chaise longue.*

She had no wish to dance. She just wanted to see the Duke, to talk to him, make him understand, and stop him from being angry with her any longer.

She remembered what the Doctor had said and was sure he would repeat it to the Duke who would realise that had she not been beside him Harry Goring would have killed him.

It had been a clever way to murder his cousin, knowing that it would be difficult in the general confusion of a big shoot to know who had fired a dangerous shot.

What was more, because the Prince of Wales was present, every effort would have been made to hush up the disastrous consequences of the so-called "accident," so that the publicity would not affect His Royal Highness in any way.

'Captain Goring was clever, very clever!'

Oletha thought, 'and because he has failed, I suppose he will try . . . again.'

She knew then the agony of loving somebody who was in danger, knowing that another time she would not be there to save the Duke.

Martha came back into the room.

"Never before in all my born days have I known anything like this happen!" she exclaimed in a scolding voice which told Oletha she was really upset. "From what the Doctor tells me you might've been killed, and what would we have done then?"

"There would have been . . . nothing you . . . could do!" Oletha replied weakly.

"I always did hate guns and anything to do with them," Martha said sharply. "Now I'll get you into bed and you'll not leave it until tomorrow morning."

"No, I will stay where I am," Oletha answered. "I am all right now that the pellets have been removed, and my neck only hurts a little."

"It's been a shock," Martha said, "and bed's the best place for you."

When she saw that Oletha had no intention of agreeing with her, she tidied the ermine lined rug she had over her knees and went away to make her a "nice cup of tea."

"That's what you need to make you feel better," she said sharply, and Oletha agreed because she knew that Martha believed it was a panacea for all ills.

As she expected, a little while after the Doctor had left her father came to see her.

"You are all right, my dearest?" he enquired.

"Quite all right, Papa. There were only three pellets, but I must admit they stung like a thousand wasps!"

"I cannot understand how it happened."

"What did the Duke say?" Oletha enquired.

"I have not had a chance to speak to him," the Colonel replied. "I did hear someone say that the keepers caught a man in the wood who should not have been there."

Oletha felt she had a dozen questions to ask, but she knew her father would not have the answers and after a little while he said he must go and dress for dinner.

"I think it would be wise for you to stay where you are," he said, "although I am sorry you must miss the dance."

"Perhaps I will join you later," Oletha replied, "I will see how I feel."

"That sounds sensible!" her father exclaimed, "and I will come back and see you before I go down to dinner."

He left her and Oletha waited.

She was hoping the Duke would ask to see her and when he did not come she supposed he expected her to be brave enough to join the guests for dinner.

She ate a little of the delicious dishes that were

brought up to her, but she was disappointed and depressed.

Only when she knew that everybody in the house would now be in the big Dining-Room where they were to be joined by a number of friends from the neighbourhood, did she go to bed as Martha wanted her to do.

What was the point, she asked herself, of putting on one of her new gowns and going down to the Ball-Room if the Duke would not dance with her and perhaps, even though she had saved his life, not even look at her?

"No decent Englishman would ever ask you to marry him!"

Oletha could hear her father saying those words and they repeated and re-repeated themselves until she felt, like the pellets from Harry Goring's gun, they were embedded in her heart.

"I'm going down for my supper now, Miss Oletha. Is there anything you wants?" Martha enquired.

Oletha wanted to reply that she only wanted one thing—to see the Duke. But aloud she said:

"Nothing, thank you, Martha. I will try to sleep."

"The best thing you could do," Martha approved.

She turned out all the lights except the one by the bedside. Then Oletha was alone.

She lay back against the pillows, finding it

more comfortable being half upright rather than lying flat.

She wondered if the Duke would notice she was not at the dinner-table, and she thought miserably that perhaps he was too busy enjoying himself with his friends to even give her a passing thought.

"I love him, and I shall love him all my life!" she whispered. "There will never be anyone else who could make me feel as he did, that we were one, and that we had belonged to each other since the beginning of time."

She went over in her mind everything they had said to each other, and once again felt that inexpressible rapture when he kissed her and she knew their love was, as he had said, an incomparable magic.

She heard the door open and thought Martha had returned sooner than she had expected.

Then she heard the unmistakable sound of the key turning in the lock and turned her head in astonishment to see the Duke coming towards her.

Wearing his decorations he looked as resplendent as he had been last night, but she could only look at his eyes knowing she would see in them what he felt for her.

He came nearer until he stood at her side and as he did so, her hands went out towards him and she said in a pleading little voice that broke:

"F—forgive me . . . please . . . forgive me! I know . . . you are . . . angry . . . but I must try to make you . . . understand."

For a moment the Duke did not move, then her hands were in his and he said:

"All I can understand at the moment is that you saved my life. How could you do anything so wonderful?"

"I did not even have . . . time to . . . think," Oletha answered. "I knew that he intended to . . . kill you and that I must . . . somehow prevent . . . it."

"Which you did."

He sat down on the bed holding her hands in his.

"How could you be so perceptive and so quick?" he asked. "At the same time how could you risk your own life?"

There was a note in his voice and a look in his eyes that made Oletha feel her misery was fading away.

She held on very tightly to his hands as if she was afraid he would leave her, and as if he understood he said:

"I dared not come to you until the men were drinking their port."

"You mean you have . . . left them in the . . . Dining-Room?"

"I instructed one of the servants to tell me there was somebody who wished to see me urgently, so I managed to escape."

"I . . . wanted to see you . . . I wanted it . . . desperately!"

"I was aware of that," the Duke said simply, "and, my darling, you have a lot of explaining to do."

He saw her eyes widen. Then she said a little incoherently:

"Y—you will . . . not be . . . angry with me?"

"How could I be after what you have done?" he asked.

"But you were . . . angry when you . . . knew who I . . . was?"

"Very, very angry!" he agreed.

"I realised Lady Grayson must have . . . told you . . . before I . . . arrived."

"It never seemed quite real that you were only a Curator's daughter. I could not believe there was another woman with the unusual name of Oletha, of the same age and who looked, I was told, exquisitely beautiful."

Oletha drew in her breath.

"I wanted to . . . see what you were . . . like. Papa said that no . . . decent Englishman would ever . . . marry me, and I could not . . . bear to be . . . married for my . . . money."

The Duke did not speak and her fingers tightened on his as she said with a little cry:

"You will . . . marry me? Please . . . marry me. If you refuse to do so . . . I shall just want to

. . . d–die . . . for I cannot live without . . . you."

"Do you mean that?" the Duke asked.

"You know I mean it," Oletha said. "I love you and I have never suffered such . . . agony and been as . . . unhappy as I have been since I arrived here . . . when you would not look at me . . . or speak to me."

"It was cruel of me," the Duke admitted, "but I was wildly, crazily in love with a lovely girl who had found me the books that I hoped would give me the money I needed immediately, and I think that later with her help we could make Gore self-supporting."

There was a little pause, then Oletha said:

"She . . . still wants to . . . help you . . . if you will . . . have her."

She thought the Duke hesitated and she said desperately:

"Please . . . please forget that I have . . . anything to offer you except my . . . heart. Surely that means more than . . . anything else?"

"That is exactly what it does," the Duke answered. "The only thing that is of real importance is your heart, my lovely one, and the fact that you are an indivisible part of me and without you I am no longer a whole or complete man."

As he spoke his lips were on hers.

He kissed her very gently and tenderly as if he was afraid to hurt her.

But to Oletha once again he carried her up into the sky, and there was all the wonder and the rapture that she had known before, only it was even more intense, more wonderful because she thought she had lost it forever.

Only when the Duke raised his head did she say because she wanted to be re-assured:

"You will . . . marry me? Tell me you . . . will!"

"I think that is the question I should be asking you," the Duke said with a smile. "But my precious, I think we both know that it is something that must happen because our love is too great for us to fight against it. It conquered us from the first moment we saw each other."

"In the window of the Library!" Oletha exclaimed.

"When you were deceiving me by pretending to be somebody else! How could you do anything so naughty?"

"I . . . I had to be certain of . . . what you were like before I . . . came to Gore with Papa."

The Duke gave a little sigh.

"It seems now incredible to think that I was trying frantically to think of some way to avoid taking a rich wife."

Oletha put her arms around his neck to pull his face closer to hers.

"Can we not . . . forget about my . . . money?" she pleaded. "I have always hated being . . . richer than . . . anybody else, and I know Mama . . . felt the same."

"I think if we use it to help other people and to make Gore a part of the glory of England, then it will not trouble us personally," the Duke said.

"You are . . . sure of that?" Oletha enquired, her eyes searching his face.

He was looking down at her with an expression of love in his eyes that was somehow different from the way he had ever looked at her before, and because she understood what he was thinking she said:

"It will not be my money . . . nor yours . . . but ours, because I am no longer me . . . but a part of you and you are part of me. Say that is true!"

"Of course it is, my precious one," the Duke agreed, "and because we both think the same and feel the same we will forget everything but each other and our happiness."

He gave a little laugh as he said:

"I shall be thought of as a 'Fortune-Hunter,' just as you will be thought to have made a good exchange for your millions by wearing my coronet. But it will not worry either of us what people say because we have the only thing that matters— our love!"

"You have said exactly what I wanted you to say!" Oletha cried. "Darling, wonderful Sandor! But you must be careful. Supposing, just . . . supposing Captain Goring tried to . . . kill you . . . again?"

"You knew it was Harry?" the Duke asked.

"Of course I knew it was he," Oletha answered. "I did not see him, but I knew he was the only person who had something to gain from your death."

The Duke was about to speak, but she interrupted him by saying:

"Perhaps . . . another time I will not be there to . . . protect you."

"As I will not have you worried," the Duke said, "I have made sure that Harry will not attempt to kill me a second time."

"How can you be . . . sure of . . . that?"

"He was caught in the wood by two of the keepers and although he made a fuss, saying that he had every right to be there, they brought him to the house where I spoke to him."

"What did he say?" Oletha asked.

"He tried to bluster his way out of the situation with a lot of lies, and I offered him a choice."

"What was that?"

"He can either live abroad in Paris, or anywhere else he fancies, and I will make him a very generous allowance as long as he does not return to England—or he can stay and I will tell everybody here including the Prince that he fired at me intending to kill me."

"So he accepted to go abroad."

"He knew that unless he did so he would be

ostracised by everyone in Society and he also needs the money."

The Duke smiled a little wryly.

"I am afraid, my darling, it was really your money I was offering him."

"He can have every penny I possess just so long as he is no longer a danger to you!" Oletha cried.

The Duke gave a laugh of sheer happiness.

"You are thinking of me, my precious one?"

"You know I am," she said. "I have been so terribly . . . frightened in case he would go on . . . trying to . . . kill you."

"I shall be safe because you will look after me, and I will be very insistent that you are always with me, by day and by night, my darling. Then I shall be certain to come to no harm."

"That is . . . what I want," Oletha said. "I want to be with you . . . to be close to you . . . but please . . . will you . . . kiss me now?"

She lifted her lips as she spoke and the Duke was kissing her passionately, possessively, fiercely as he had the night in the Library.

Only when he drew her a little closer and felt her wince because her neck hurt her, did he say with a note of consternation in his voice:

"Forgive me, my darling. I am being rough and hurting you. It is only because you excite me so madly!"

"I . . . want to excite you," Oletha whispered,

"and you must teach me how I can . . . do so."

"I do not think you will need many lessons," the Duke smiled. "But now, my precious, I must leave you not only because you excite me, but because if I stay I shall compromise you in the eyes of the Social World."

Oletha laughed.

"They would certainly be extremely shocked if they knew that every time you have kissed me I have only been wearing a nightgown! And also that I stayed alone with you at Gore with no chaperon."

"No-one must ever know that happened," the Duke said. "I suppose you can trust the real Curator, if there is one?"

"He is coming here on Monday," Oletha replied, "and I promise you he will not betray us. Besides, he really is only interested in books."

She paused. Then she said:

"I wondered if you really wanted to sell the Folio and the Bible if I could . . . buy them. It is because they . . . brought us . . . together that they are very, very precious to me . . . personally."

"Together we will decide what to do about them and everything else," the Duke said, "but, dearest love, I really must leave you. God knows it is an indescribable agony to do so. I would like to stay with you for hours, or better still all night, telling you how beautiful you are and kissing you from the top of your glorious golden head to the soles of your little feet."

There was a note of passion in his voice and a fire in his eyes which made Oletha put her arms around his neck again.

"I love you! I adore you!" she said. "Please ... marry me very ... quickly."

"As quickly as your father will let me," the Duke murmured.

His lips found hers and he kissed her once again until she felt as if the world whirled round them and he was lifting her into the sky.

Then when it seemed to her as if he gave her the moon and the stars so that she held them to her breast, the Duke rose to his feet.

"I have to go," he said as if he spoke to himself, then he bent down to kiss her once again and she felt the fire in his lips.

"Think of me, dream of me," he ordered, "until tomorrow when somehow we will be alone so that I can hold you in my arms."

Before she could answer he moved across the room, unlocked the door and went out.

She listened to his footsteps going down the passage, then as she felt herself pulsating with the wonder of his kisses and the glory of his love, she whispered over and over again:

"Thank You, God, Thank You ... Thank You ... !"

BARBARA CARTLAND'S NEW MAGAZINE

SPECIAL OFFER

If you love Barbara Cartland's books, you'll feel the same way about her new magazine. **Barbara Cartland's World of Romance** is the new monthly that contains an illustrated Cartland novel, the story behind the story, Barbara's personal message to readers, and many other fascinating and colorful features.

You can save $4.73 when you try an Introductory 9-month subscription. On newsstands, 9 issues cost $13.50. But with this coupon, you pay only $8.77!

Less than 98¢ an issue for nine months of the best in romantic fiction.

NO RISK: If you don't like your first copy for any reason, cancel your subscription and keep the first issue FREE. Your money will be refunded in full.

SUBSCRIBE TODAY. Just send your name and address with this coupon and $8.77 to Box BM, c/o Jove Publications, Inc., 200 Madison Avenue, New York, N. Y. 10016. Make check or m.o. payable to *World of Romance.*

SPECIAL DISCOUNT COUPON—WORTH $4.73